I0823446

METAMORPHOSIS

Nicholas Mosley

DALKEY ARCHIVE PRESS
Champaign / London / Dublin

Library of Congress Cataloging-in-Publication Data

Mosley, Nicholas, 1923-
Metamorphosis / Nicholas Mosley. -- First edition.

pages cm
ISBN 978-1-62897-024-1 (pbk. : alk. paper)
I. Title.
PR6063.O82M48 2014
823'.914--dc23

2014006777

Partially funded by the Illinois Arts Council, a state agency.

www.dalkeyarchive.com

Cover: design and composition by Mikhail Iliatov
Printed on permanent/durable acid-free paper

METAMORPHOSIS

1.

I CAME TO the cliff-top above the sea at sunset, where the light on the horizon was forcing its way through the clouds like bars in front of a window. I imagined a girl in a room behind looking down at something in the street below – a dog perhaps, or a lover, or a child she had once taken care of. This scene then switched in my mind to a painting by Giorgione in Venice which for a long time had been my favourite painting in the world – of a landscape with a walled town in the background and a stream running under a small bridge to the front, and with the broken remnant of a much larger bridge behind. At the edge of the left side of the picture there is a young man in rustic clothes standing nonchalantly leaning on a spear; he is looking towards the opposite side of the picture where a woman is seated on a rock and suckling child. She is paying no attention to the man who is watching her, but is looking out of the picture to the front, presumably in the direction of the painter. However the woman and the man seem clearly connected to one another without any indication as to what this connection might be.

This at least is how I remembered it.

I was thinking now at the cliff-top – And what is

their connection with the girl behind the window? She is there to warn them? To tell them that things are all right?

I stepped as near as I could with safety (so I felt) to the edge of the cliff, in order to look down on the beach below. What else might a girl in the sky be looking at? I had not yet been down to walk on the beach; we had only come to our rented cottage on the west coast of Ireland two days ago. The beach was wide and sandy, with evidently an extensive tide. We could play games on it, I thought – I and my stepson Peter aged twelve, and my wife Alix, and our daughter Phoebe aged three. It was not easy to find games which all of us could play; but was not that part of the game? Now, looking down on the beach some fifty feet below, there seemed to be on it some strange excrescence – a large dark growth like a carbuncle; but the shifting light made it difficult to see. Or more likely it was a depression, a cavity, something scooped out of the sand and left by the tide. But that did not make much sense. And then I found that I was taking off into space; my feet had slipped and I was grabbing behind me for a handhold but finding none. Or rather nothing but grass; which might be the hair of the girl who had managed to lean further out of her window? And perhaps the dark shape below me might be a pool into which I might splash harmlessly; or even one of those things like a trampoline on which firemen catch people jumping from windows. However, I was now managing to claw and scramble my way back to firm ground at the top of the cliff. There I lay for a moment and thought – Well what was all that about? You can play with imagination and make of it anything or nothing. But if there has been danger?

We had come to this cottage by the sea in Ireland to have a break from life in London; also I could tell myself I was doing research-work for journalism. I had in fact been doing research in libraries for a Member of Parliament who had concerns in this part of Ireland which was close to the border between North and South, and where there were reports of renewed disturbances. I had wondered about the wisdom of taking my family to such an area; but according to most official reports the so-called 'troubles' were now over, having been settled by what was known as the Good Friday Agreement. For the Member of Parliament I excavated the politics: I myself was more interested in sensing the atmosphere of a place where murderous antagonism between Catholics and Protestants was said to have been settled by an agreement called Good Friday.

I was walking back to the cottage to have supper with my family, my mind awash with what I had seen or imagined on and above the beach: why had that picture in Venice come into my head? Was that what the girl at the window in my mind had been looking at? What was that dark stain or presence on the beach? Are there connections between images that occur in one's mind and what might be going on in the outside world? I had a great friend called Johnny who had been at school and university with me and had been Alix's husband; he had trained as a neuroscientist and had become quite well known in this profession. I had concentrated more on history and philosophy and literature. We used to have long and fervent talks about how what went on in the brain might or must influence, as well as originate from, what was observed and experienced in the outside world. I would say – Physicists are now suggesting that it is the observer who is in some way responsible for the 'reality' that he observes: how can this be explained? Johnny would say – It's a way of putting it.

When I got back to the cottage there was only Alix in the kitchen-living-room. I had hoped to narrate the story of my cliff-top adventure, but my stepson Peter might be a better audience than Alix, who was liable to become overburdened with my fantasies. Peter was Johnny's child, and had become interested in what had interested his father. I said to Alix 'Have the children gone to bed?' She said 'No they're in the cowshed.'

I said 'The cowshed!'

She said 'One of the cows is in calf. It's due any minute.'

I thought – Oh well, my story has not got a chance.

I said 'Can you remember what that picture in Venice was called – the one by Giorgione that I love so much? There's a man with a spear on one side and a woman nursing a child on the other. They're aware of each other, and yet at the same time not.'

Alix said 'The Tempest.'

I said 'The Tempest! It's so calm and serene.'

She said 'Yes, and you had one of your great theories about that.'

Oh yes, I had held forth about – what on earth – How if you cared about someone you had also to distance yourself from them in order to allow them their freedom; but then this also brought into play some sort of control. Could what enabled this be imagined as a tempest?

My daughter Phoebe came whirling into the room from the garden. She did a fragile dervish-like dance; then said 'Jersey's had a calf! She's called Jumper!'

It came into my mind to say – Jersey's not the name of an individual cow. But I said 'Jumper's a good name!'

Phoebe said 'It is! It is!' Then – 'And I helped pull it out!' She dashed out of the room again.

Alix, by the stove, was saying 'Then you'd better come and wash your hands.'

I was thinking – But should or shouldn't one follow Phoebe to the cowshed to see she is all right?

Alix said 'Do they really pull it out?'

I said 'They can do if it gets stuck.'

Alix might now have said 'How do you know such things.' But she said 'They're all very sweet with her in the cowshed. And Peter's there to see she's all right.'

I said nonchalantly, in the manner of what I imagined was that of the man in the painting with a spear – 'I once worked on a farm.'

Alix brought some soup over to the table. I sat at my place at the head in a high-backed chair. I was thinking – And a birth is like a tempest, so beautiful and yet so bloody.

Alix said 'Mr Brewster thinks the troubles between North and South may be starting up again.'

I was going to say – Who's Mr Brewster? But Alix went on – 'He was saying our beach is sometimes used by smugglers.'

So I was thinking – So that was that strange dark object! and I was beginning – 'I was walking by the cliff this evening when – .' But then Peter came in from the garden, so I stopped. But had I not been thinking that Peter would be a good audience for my story?

Peter is a stammerer; which makes him often

reluctant to speak, but also seem sometimes unusually attentive to other people's stories. But this makes him also aware, surely, of the frequent inanity of them?

Peter eventually managed – 'Mr Brewster says there was a whale washed up on the beach last night.'

I was thinking – So that was it! But still – Who on earth is Mr Brewster?

Alix said 'Where's Phoebe?'

Phoebe shouted 'Here!' and jumped out from behind Peter's back, where she had been hiding.

I said 'Who's Mr Brewster?' Then I thought – How many times have I said this? So I began again – 'I was walking by the cliff-top just now and there was something huge on the sand – '

Phoebe said 'It came out with a whoosh!'

Alix said 'He knows all the local gossip.'

Peter said fluently 'They say the beach is used by insurgents.'

I thought – What an odd word!

Alix said again 'Now come and wash your hands.'

I was wondering – Could one smuggle explosives in the belly of a whale? Like Jonah? Jonah was an insurgent? But then I wouldn't have been able to bounce –

A man with a large round face put his head round the edge of the open door from the garden, then withdrew it quickly. The others did not seem to have noticed.

I thought – But I can't ask again – Was that Mr Brewster?

Peter was saying 'I didn't put my hand in.'

Phoebe was saying 'I did!'

Peter said 'She touched the rope.'

Alix looked at me enquiringly.

I said 'They sometimes use a rope if they need to reach the front feet of the calf inside the cow.' I was thinking – But that does sounds a bit unlikely.

Peter said 'Do they feel pain?'

Alix said 'Yes I think one always feels pain, but that's part of what makes it seem so all right afterwards.'

I was thinking – That strange barred light might have meant there was a tempest out at sea?

I said 'Was that Mr Brewster who put his head round the door?'

They turned and stared at me blankly. I thought – All right, all right!

Alix said 'Now come and have supper.'

I thought – We take such trouble to bring things to birth, anyway, and then we eat them.

We ate in silence for a while. Then Peter said without a stammer 'What are the troubles?'

I said 'Oh the troubles, the troubles. In Ireland they were between Catholics from the south and Protestants and English in the north, and they both called themselves Christians, but they each seemed to need an enemy, so it was easiest for them to be enemies to one another.'

After an effort Peter said 'But weren't they both supposed to love their enemies?'

I said 'Yes, but what if what they both loved was fighting.'

Alix got up from the table and went to the sink. I imagined her thinking – That's not so very clever.

Then after a while Peter said 'Is that what my father was on about?'

I said 'Well, he thought it should be possible to find a way of handling the dottiness of human nature. He was a scientist.'

Peter said 'You mean controlling it.'

I said 'Well, making it work.'

I thought – I should go and put my arm round Alix at the sink.

But also, did I not need to be on my own for a bit, to be able to think about this.

When I and Johnny, Peter's father, had been at university he had been doing biology and physics and I had been doing history and philosophy (have I said this before? I shall say it again). Johnny's passion was to understand the workings of the human brain; and then if possible to try to do something to change these. When one looked out on the world – this was a favourite topic in our talks with one another – one saw the madness of humans; but the way people sought to do something about this was to gather various notable humans together to talk, to confer, to argue; but by doing this the madness was multiplied like bits of shrapnel being crammed into a cluster bomb. The madness was in the nature of the human individual, the human brain. How by gathering humans together could humanity be changed?

There was a new fashion however establishing itself in neuroscience, the science of the brain, so Johnny had informed me: this was to see the human brain in terms of a computer – both in studying its actual form, or by getting a computer or system of computers to model the brain – and by doing this, all right, learn not only to understand the brain but also to change it. And if I looked sceptical, Johnny would say – Well what else is there to do?' Take brains out of living people to manipulate them? Just go on being bonkers?

I would sometimes think – Or hope to change the soil into which some unusual living seed might fall and flourish?

We would both agree that there was not much point in bringing God back into this – or whatever it is that science now recognises is around or above nature. What had once been called God didn't seem to have wanted to arrange how humans evolve: he had given them freedom, and evidently wanted them to be responsible for their own evolution. If they had once needed or wanted to fight one another, all right; but now this had come to seem so distasteful, could they not learn from this what else they might like? God could scatter a few suggestions, after all –

But this was what he had done?

I was remembering this sort of conversation when I became aware that I was on my own in the kitchen. It seemed that Alix and Phoebe must have gone up to bed. The cottage had only two small bedrooms; Peter insisted that he preferred anyway to sleep in the garden in his tent.

I thought I might go out and lie on the grass and watch the stars emerge in the night sky. Or should I go and make sure that things were all right with Alix?

Make love with Alix?

Humans are not computers.

2.

In the morning I thought I would set up a chair and table in a corner of the garden and try to work there. I had learned so much from Johnny, and he used to say he had learnt so much under questioning from me. And now Johnny had gone on a journey and had seemed just to disappear. So was it not now up to me to sort out what we had said, and try to write it down? But as Johnny had so often said – That's the key point: you can't really put this sort of thing into words.

What sort of thing?

Johnny had teamed up with various groups of people who were experimenting with treating the brain as a computer, with special reference to the question of whether, or how, human characteristics might be changed. But then – how can one search for what might be a desirable change in the brain by using one's brain as the agency of search? Johnny would say – All right, if you can't put this into words, then at least go out into the world and observe how people in fact do or don't change. I had thought – And by this affect the chance of change?

He had said 'You know what physicists are now saying about the observer determining as it were the event or experiment that they observe?'

I said 'Yes.'

He had said 'So what about free will.'

I had said 'Free will is in choosing to observe and to be aware of observing. This results in things that may be either according to one's will or not.'

He had said 'Ah, then what's that according to? Genes and chance?'

I had said 'Those are words.'

He had said 'Well, what about meaning? That's not just a word.'

I had thought – You mean, it might be meaningless – or like a work of art?

Like that painting?

I was struggling not only with my thoughts but with a chair and small table and my laptop into the garden, when I noticed that the flap of Peter's tent was open and he was not inside. I thought – Yes, I would have liked to have talked with him about this; I could have asked him something about Johnny. Then I realised he was just behind me, which made me jump.

Peter said 'Sorry.'

'Oh that's all right!'

He was wearing shorts and gym shoes. His bedding in the tent was so tidy that it looked as though it had not been slept in.

He said 'There really is a whale on the beach.'

I said 'Have you been down to see?'

He said 'There's quite a crowd. They seem to be trying to cut it open. Or drag it back into the sea.'

I said 'You mean it's still alive?' I thought – Or it really might be full of explosives?

He said 'No I don't think so.' He seemed to be watching me as if there were something further I might do.

I said 'Wait, and I'll come back with you.' I thought – I mean, just as far as the cliff-top.

I left the garden chair and table, and dithered about what to do with the laptop. I often wanted to hurl it away. I chose to drop it off in the house. On the way out of the garden and on to the long slope to the cliff-top, I said to Peter 'Did your father used to talk to you about the work he was doing?'

Peter said 'Yes he sometimes did.'

I said 'What sort of things did he say?'

Peter said 'But if you can't choose to change human nature, what can you do?' Then with a bit of a stammer – 'I mean, that stuff we were talking about last night.'

I said 'Oh yes.' Then – 'Well you can choose to change yourself, your circumstances, up to a point. And then other things may change in such a way themselves.'

'But can you change yourself if you are like a computer?'

'But you're only like a computer if you choose to

treat yourself like a computer. Up to a point.'

'What point.'

'Beyond which you can tell what has meaning and what has not.'

Peter seemed to be thinking about this. Then – 'But isn't that just genes and chance?'

I said 'Well that's what you have to find out.'

'How?'

'By looking. By watching. By remembering. Not turning things away.'

'What?'

'Whatever turns up.'

'Which may have nothing to do with you.'

'Well either it has or it hasn't.'

Peter said 'And that's what – ? What you find – ? If you put yourself in the way of – ?' And then fluently – 'And that's what my father was doing?'

I said 'I hope that's what he's doing now.'

It struck me suddenly that perhaps Peter might think his father was dead.

I thought – Oh Johnny, for God's sake, Johnny!

We were coming to the cliff-top; there was quite a crowd round the large dark object on the beach below. This seemed smaller than I remembered it, but it did at least now look like a fish. The evening sun must have added shadows to it. And a stranded whale is surely a rarity on this coast. The crowd around it seemed to have done with it whatever they wanted to do (cutting it open? really?) and now seemed to be fastening a rope round its tail. Peter said 'Are whales' brains like computers?' I said 'I don't think so.' Peter said 'I read somewhere that they talk to one another by singing.' I thought – So that might have meaning! Like Tristan and Isolde dying on their rocky beach.

Down below among the crowd there was a truck to which was being fastened the other end of the rope from the whale's tail. I thought – They are going to pull it back into the sea as a cover-up? But everything is now seen as a cover-up. Then after Tristan and Isolde, one can go and have dinner.

But this doesn't seem to have much meaning.

Do any of the troubles in Ireland have a meaning?

Or are they just passing the time because there's not much to look forward to for dinner.

Then from above us and to one side there was a crack like that of a bullet from a rifle.

I thought – But this is still ridiculous.

I considered explaining – If a bullet is fired at you, you hear two bangs, the first is of the bullet going overhead, and the second that of the gun from which it was fired. Like this you can judge distance.

Alix might even say this time – How do you know such things!

Then I saw that Alix and Phoebe were coming

up the long green slope from the cottage towards us. I thought of yelling 'Get down!' But wouldn't this make things even more ridiculous? But of course it was serious! *Was* it?

Peter said 'Well that wasn't a computer.'

I said 'No.' Though I thought – Of course it could be.

Peter said 'Have you been in a war?'

I said 'I was once in Lebanon.'

'Was that a war?'

'Not really.' So then I began – 'When a bullet is fired at you, you first hear – '

But Alix had stopped and was crouching about a hundred yards away; Phoebe was behind her. I did not want to turn my eyes away too long from trying to understand what was happening on the beach.

Then Peter said 'What happened to my father, do you know?'

I said 'I'm sure he's all right.'

Peter said 'How?'

I said 'I can't explain. But I think I'd know.'

I thought – Perhaps all this stuff is happening just so that I can say that to him.

Alix was moving. She was half running half crawling up the slope towards where there was a sort of cairn of stones at the top. She was holding Phoebe with one hand, and holding a doll in front of her with the other as if it were a weapon or a shield.

I said to Peter 'Do you think your father might have died?'

Peter said 'It's the sort of thing he used to talk about.'

'What?'

'Something about to be properly alive you had also to know at the same time you might be dead.'

The cairn was about equidistant from where Peter and I were crouching, and where Alix and Phoebe had now stopped again. I thought – What in God's name do any of us think we're doing? I said to Peter 'Stay here.' Peter said 'No, I want to come with you.' I thought – You take a risk, yes; but what's a risk and what isn't.

I began to run, still crouching, towards Alix and Phoebe; then in the direction of the cairn, which they were now again moving towards. I was trying to remember that phrase – In life we are in death – or whatever.

I should remember to say to Peter – Your father just thought he had some special things to try out.

We all arrived at the cairn at the same time. Alix was now carrying Phoebe. I thought – Presumably we had in mind that a cairn provides shelter. Not all that ridiculous. But then one can all be caught at the same time; but had there really been a rifle shot? From the beach? Aimed at the beach? I should have paid more attention. Alix had put Phoebe on the ground and Phoebe was jumping up and down singing 'We won!'

The cairn was a circular wall of stones about three feet high with no top to it. Peter was leaning over the wall peering inside. He said quietly 'No one wins.'

Alix looked over the wall of the cairn. She remained as if carefully studying what was inside.

Peter lifted Phoebe up so that she could see inside. Phoebe said 'Mr Brewster Rooster!'

There was a man in the cairn lying as if resting with his back propped against the wall at the back so that he was facing the sea. I thought – But is or isn't that the man who put his head round the door? Then – But surely he couldn't have fired the shot because the sound – But he did have a small-calibre rifle resting between his knees.

Phoebe said 'Cock-a-doodle-do!'

The barrel of the rifle was pointing up beneath his chin. What was that joke they used to do about suicides in films – What happened? – I missed.

But then the point surely is, as I had thought, that the event is anyway ridiculous.

Alix was saying 'That's not Mr Brewster.'

Phoebe was saying 'It is!'

Peter was saying 'Don't wake him up.'

The man in the cairn was wearing thick denims

with a woolly hat pulled down on his head. He opened one eye and saw Phoebe and said 'Fucking hell!'

Phoebe said 'Fucky Nell!'

Alix said 'Were you on the look-out for the whale?'

I thought what might be better would have been – Were you out after rabbits?

Peter had wandered back to look over the top of the cliff. He now came running to us again and said 'There are police down below.'

The man in the cairn had sat up and was now crouching theatrically with the muzzle of his rifle on top of the wall facing the sea.

I thought – Or is one expected to say – We haven't seen you.

Peter said 'They don't seem to have found anything interesting.'

Alix said 'Let's go home then.'

The man said 'Yes, you go home.'

Phoebe said 'Me want to stay.'

The man turned his head and seemed to consider us for the first time carefully. Then he laughed and said 'Little lady, I'll be waiting for you.' Then he stood and vaulted nimbly over the wall of the cairn and walked away down the slope in the opposite direction to that of the cottage, with the rifle on its strap over his shoulder. We watched him as if we were waiting for the next event to happen.

Alix said 'What was all that about?'

I said 'I don't think it was about anything.'

Alix said 'But it went all right?'

I said 'Yes.'

The man had gone about fifty yards and was almost over the brow of the hill when he suddenly flung his arms up and disappeared out of sight.

Peter said 'I didn't hear anything.'

I said 'No.'

I thought – Perhaps he just needs to explain to someone that he sprained his ankle.

Alix waited for a while, then went in the direction where the man had gone. I found myself once more on the point of shouting 'Get back!' but there seemed even less point now than ever. So why not let the thing take its course. Peter lifted Phoebe down from the cairn and we followed Alix down the slope. The man who had been in the cairn was lying face down with his rifle in one hand stretched out in front of him, again theatrically. Alix knelt by him. I thought – But people usually need excuses for almost everything, yes?

The man said quietly 'Git sway from me ye daft buggers!'

Alix said 'No we're here to help you.'

Peter said 'I don't think he's hurt.'

Phoebe shouted 'You're not hurt!'

The man said 'Am I not then?' He felt his sides and legs. Then he pushed himself onto his feet, once more nimbly. Then one leg seemed to give way and he almost collapsed again. He laughed and said 'It's a fine distinction.'

I thought – What Johnny was on about was that stuff about Schrödinger's Cat.

Then, as if explaining to Peter – This was a thought-experiment thought up by physicists –

A woman was emerging from some trees at the bottom of the slope. She stood with her hands on her hips looking up at us. Alix said 'Did you trip and twist your ankle?' The man said 'Bejasus you're stickers.' Alix said 'Put your arm round my shoulder then.' Peter took hold of his other hand, and the man suddenly sang loudly 'Come fill your glasses to the brim, all ye who love renown.' I thought – Oh yes, and that goes on to rhyme with something about the harp and crown. We stumbled on down the hill.

I thought – Does that mean he's a Protestant?

Peter said to the man 'Who was it firing?'

The man sang – 'I'll drink a toast to every man – '

I remembered that I had promised to try to explain to Peter about Schrödinger's Cat – the thought-experiment conjured up by some modern physicists to try to make a nonsense of things thought up by other even more modern physicists – the idea that at the heart of matter, or at the outer reaches of the universe, something could be either, or both (or perhaps neither?) a particle and/or a wave at the same time; in fact perhaps all apparent opposites could be either one or the other or both at the same time; and what or which something was thought to be, depended on the view of the experimenter or observer – had I got that right? So a cat was shut up in a box – and so on and so on, but this could wait. However if the whole point had been to make a nonsense of science by scientists, why had they wanted to do this? In the experiment with the cat, the cat supposedly could be said to be both alive and dead at the same time – but was this trying to make a nonsense of science or of life? Or making sense of life? Why not?

We were stumbling down the hill. We were getting closer to the woman who had appeared at the edge of the wood. She was standing with her hands on her hips looking at us sternly. When we were close to her she said to the man with the rifle 'So you're alive ye daft bugger.'

The man said 'Is that so.'

The woman was saying 'Who're your friends?'

The man said 'Ay, who are ye?'

Alix said 'We're from the cottage.'

The woman said 'And a lot of good that'll do ye.'

Phoebe said 'Jersey's had a calf.'

The woman said 'Has she now.'

The man said to me 'They steal our sheep.'

I thought of saying – Do they now?

The woman said 'Ay, but they're not from here.'

Phoebe said 'She's called Jumper.'

Peter said 'Where are they from?'

The woman said 'That's a good name.'

Alix said 'Well we don't want to keep you any longer.'

The woman said to the man 'Come in and we'll warm you.'

As we walked away I was thinking – Well that did the trick. But what trick?

This time it was I who said to Alix 'What was all that about?'

And Alix said 'I don't think about anything really.'

We walked round the edge of the wood till we could see our cottage in the distance. I was trying to get straight in my mind – A cat is shut up in a box with a radioactive particle (or a wave?) that has a 50-50 chance of decaying within a certain time and releasing a poison that would kill the cat. But until someone opens the box and looks in, the cat could not be said to be either alive or dead but both at the same time, because of the 50-50 chances, or were they scientifically 100-100 –

Peter and I had wandered ahead of the others.

Peter said 'You were going to tell me something.'

I said 'Oh yes. About Schrödinger's cat.'

Peter said 'Yes.'

I said 'Well scientists were just trying to score off one another. That's what scientists do. There was an experiment that one set of people thought up to make a nonsense of what another set of people had thought up, which had made it seem that a cat might be shut up in a box and could be both alive and dead at the same time, until someone opened the box and looked in.'

'And could it?'

'That was a way of putting it.'

I thought – That's what Johnny used to say.

Peter said 'So it's up to oneself to look.'

I said 'Yes exactly.'

We wandered along. We were now out of the wood. Peter said 'But why do scientists want to score off one another?'

I said 'That's just what people do, isn't it?'

Peter said 'Then isn't it what people do that needs to be changed?'

I said 'Yes indeed.'

I was thinking again – Oh Johnny, for God's sake, Johnny!

Peter said 'And that was what my father was on about?'

I said 'Yes I believe so.'

Then I remembered Johnny saying something like – And of course God was known specifically as being both alive and dead at the same time –

So why on earth do Christians at least need to score off one another?

We were coming to the few ramshackle buildings of the farmyard. I thought – They would make someone a nice home. Peter had become silent. Alix and Phoebe were coming up behind. I was going back in my memory to the first time I had seen Alix: she had just become Johnny's wife and it was said they had married because she had become pregnant –

Peter was saying 'But you're saying no one's actually done this experiment.'

I said 'No, it was a move in a game. But the important thing, as you say, is how to change human nature.'

Peter said 'I remember my father saying something about Bible stories being both true and untrue.'

I said 'Oh goodness, yes!'

Peter said 'You have them in mind. And then you open the box and look in. And they are or are not.'

I thought – And that's because of God? That really is very clever!

Peter said 'Do you think that's what my father's trying to do?'

There was a small herd of cattle being herded across the road in front of us. Phoebe, who had caught up with us with Alix, ran forwards shouting 'Go home!' Alix was saying 'They are going home.'

Phoebe said 'They're going to be eaten!'

Alix said 'Not yet.'

I thought – You mean in the end we're all eaten? Like God?

Peter and I were coming to the garden gate at the front of our cottage. I was thinking – But the way of dealing with all this is just to carry on, trying to be aware of what is going on both outside and in the mind; and then what is meant to happen, which may be quite different from what you plan to happen, may happen.

Peter said 'Have you got anything I could read?'

I said 'Yes, hold on.' We went into the cottage.

I said 'I've got a book just here, which I packed at the last minute, which tries to connect modern science with sorts of Eastern mysticism.'

Peter said 'Mysticism!'

I said 'That's how you might see things if you open the box.'

Peter said 'Thanks.'

I said 'It's been good to talk.'

Peter held the book against his chest as if it might be a protection, or recording a heartbeat.

3.

THE FIRST TIME I had seen Alix was when she had just married Johnny, and it was said that they had married because she had been made pregnant by him. I had not been at the hurried wedding, but there was a small party soon afterwards to which many of his friends came; and Alix of course was there but also seemed to be not quite part of it; however, not just because of her pregnancy surely? She spent most of the time preparing snacks or drinks in the kitchen, where she could be seen through an open hatch moving sedately here and there like a leaf in the backwater of a stream. Or she was seated quite still with her hands in her lap and not seeming to be doing anything: yet there was some vibration coming from her, or was it being projected from me? Oh yes, I was falling in love with her. I had in some way been in love with Johnny I suppose, during our years at boarding school when there had been no girls around; and I had even hopped into bed with him once or twice. But now to love Alix was surely impossible, however much it might be desired – and even psychologically explicable. In appearance Alix was the opposite of Johnny – short and fair-haired; her presence held as if in the framework of a painting.

In the next room Johnny was saying 'But when in science has there ever been any attempt to say anything about free will? And indeed why bother, if we're all like computers.'

And someone was saying 'Don't you believe in free will then?'

And Johnny was saying 'Oh yes, it's everywhere. But you don't believe you can control it.'

And someone said 'And what does that mean?'

Johnny said 'You can't tell a wall to fall down and it will fall down. You may have some freedom in what concerns you.'

Someone said 'And what does that mean.'

Johnny said 'I suppose you try it and find out.'

I had gone upstairs to the small bedroom in the cottage to write this. The bedroom was supposed to be Phoebe's, but I squeezed into it in order to work when it seemed not warm enough to sit outside. I was having my usual troubles with my computer: small rectangular notices would emerge from the recesses of the screen containing requests or instructions that I did not understand. And as if in response to my stupidity the print would then become huge or tiny, or disappear half off the screen on one side. And when I fiddled there would eventually be a notice – 'This is a Read Only Copy. Do you wish to continue?' I would want to reply – No, I wish to throw you out of the window. But then I would think – Am I not talking to myself?

I had once been with a colleague of Johnny's and had asked him – It sometimes seems to me that when I get over-excited about what I am writing the electronics of my brain transfer themselves to the electronica of the computer and so it goes phut – but is not this absurd? And Johnny's colleague had looked thoughtful for a moment, and then had said 'Not necessarily, no.' So now when there seemed to be a misunderstanding in communication between my computer and me, I tried to make myself think – But my dear computer, maybe you are trying to make me realise I am on the wrong track; there is something I should be remembering, be writing about, and am not. Is this realisation part of what is referred to as loving one's enemy?

And it was true that recently I had been wondering – But there is, yes, a great chunk of my life that I am leaving out of this story, or leaving till later, but why? With the best of intentions, perhaps; but do not these often cover up what might be of importance? The making a fool of oneself, perhaps; or imagining that one has been involved in what Johnny and Peter might call a 'Biblical' story? Oh really! But all right, my dear computer; I'm only trying to make the best of what happens; and now can you please help me with what may be carried on.

*

One of my first jobs of any importance as a journalist was to be sent out to East Africa to do a 'human interest' story about the drought that was causing widespread famine and pestilence in the area; in particular a lethal outbreak among children of hydrocephalus or water-on-the-brain. This offer of an interesting job happened soon after the party at which for the first time I had seen Alix, and had taken on board as it were her pregnancy and her marriage to Johnny, as well as my seeming to fall in love with her. I thought – Perhaps I will be going out to Africa to die: perhaps I have already got water on the brain.

In the vast barren landscape near the border of Kenya with Somalia there was a camp for refugees that stretched for miles. Here hundreds of thousands had gathered, mostly women and children, and many fleeing from the chaos in Somalia in the hope of finding sustenance and assistance. One of the agencies active here was the Care for Children Fund, which provided me with a guide and an interpreter; I had my own hired truck from Nairobi, in which I intended to sleep and work. But the scale and extremity of the disaster was hard to describe: what does one say, what does one do, about such catastrophe? Squat tents and shelters made of sticks and bits of cloth were stuck everywhere like patches of dressing on an overall wounded earth. Families with mothers and children, or just children on their own, spilled out of these and lay like drops of puss or blood. I did not know how to write about this; I did not know how to think about it; I could only think – But what does one do. My mind kept going back, or forward, to and fro, to any family I might have had, or not had, with Alix. Just before I had left England I had had a conversation with Johnny and he had said – Yes, Alix wouldn't consider an abortion, and I thought she was quite right. And she had been a virgin, and so – . And so, I thought, aren't you lucky! And Johnny said 'Aren't I lucky.'

I got all the information I could about the camp. I made notes in a notebook and rather missed the companionship of my computer. I found myself thinking – Goddam it, God, how can you let people call you good and let all this happen. To children, I mean, to babies. And then a woman came crawling headfirst out of a small semi-circular tent and she was clasping a baby in one arm as she crawled, so that the baby's head was just under her own. And I thought – They are like conjoined twins coming out of a womb. Then the woman struggled to her feet, still holding the baby, and the baby's head as I stared at it seemed to have more awareness than her own. The woman, who looked European, was staring back at me. She said 'Are you

English?' I said 'Yes.' She said 'Will you marry me?' I said 'Yes.'

She told me what seemed to be necessary about herself and the baby while I went with her and the baby to the Care for Children hut. The baby had been born a few days ago and there were many of the signs, yes, of it having hydrocephalus or water on the brain. It could not be treated properly here, but there was every chance that it could be dealt with and eventually cured in England – they put in a tube or something, and drained it out. But she had no papers, no documents; she wasn't exactly English, no. But she had been working for the Care for Children people for some time; and she had become enormously fond of the mother of this baby, and then of the baby, yes; no she couldn't exactly describe why. Did I want her to try? I said – No. But the mother was too far gone with malnutrition and her own diseases; she had lived long enough to show her gladness for the baby; and then just a few minutes ago had died. But before this the woman who was now talking to me had promised to do everything she could for the baby – for its survival and its life.

She was now saying 'It doesn't have to be a proper marriage. We can get it done by one of the odd local sects here, I can do all the arrangements and the paperwork, and there'll be no lasting evidence of it. You don't have to worry. All I need is your name on the passports to get to England, you don't even have to know my name. And after we're in England you need never see or hear from me or about the baby again. I promise you. In fact if you don't agree to this, I won't embark on it. It wouldn't be fair on you.'

I said 'Why are you embarking on it?'

She said 'I've told you, I can't explain.' Then – 'Oh yes, and can you do the air fares?'

I said 'Yes I'll do the air fares.'

She said 'Oh all right. There are all these millions of starving children and what do we do about it, what can you do about it – Do you know that thing – what is it – In as much as ye have done it to one of the least of these, ye have done it to all – who was it who said that, was it Jesus?'

I said 'I expect so.' Then – 'What is your name?'

She said 'Joanna.'

*

This was as far as I got with this first time of trying to write about Joanna. My computer had behaved impeccably. By the end I found I was nearly in tears.

I thought – Give it a rest. What was the stuff that was happening now?

Joanna had been like something that happened

in another dimension. The one that held what made sense of outer spaces and the stars.

And had I not agreed that the whole incident should be forgotten?

But one does not have control of such things. They keep coming back, forcing their way in.

There was an evening when Alix and I had said we would go and have a drink in the local pub with the man we had come across in the cairn. Why on earth had we agreed to this? I had been working in my small upstairs room in the cottage.

What I had not yet mentioned about Joanna was the extraordinary force and impact of her personality. The day I had spent with her watching her as she moved around the camp making arrangements about leaving, she seemed to weave around and through and between people outwitting them like an expert footballer among novices. People would occasionally try to delay her by plucking at her sleeve; she would ignore them as if they were flies. The other quality I have not yet mentioned is her looks; she was a tall striking girl with dark hair like an Amazon; an opposite I suppose to Alix; and thus not really my type?

But anyway, the whole style of the experience in which Joanna and I had been involved seemed impossible to put into words. We followed the plan she had outlined – we attended a ceremony with drums and dancing in a tribal part of the country, and a man like a witch-doctor gave a blessing that was said to signify marriage – and why should it not? Joanna handled any paperwork required in Nairobi on her own; I did not know how she did this and I did not ask. Of course there were risks involved; but was not this part of the style required?

And throughout there was the wide-eyed as if sun-tanned baby – but how much do men usually care or dare to think about babies? I had imagined (but had we ever talked about this?) that Joanna and the Care for Children people would know how to get the baby suitably adopted when, or if, its cure had been successfully completed. Or might she even wish to look after the baby herself? However, all this did seem necessary, even possible, to put out of mind. Was not this part of what was natural for humans, I mean? Just experience or getting on with things. Until other things lumbered their way into one's mind.

That evening, as I have said, after I had been writing this in the cottage, we were on our way to the pub for an evening that was likely to be at the opposite but facing segment of the circle of things – almost too boring to put into words. Oh was or was not the man Mr Brewster; was he a protestant or a catholic; was he a joker or a terrorist; what did the troubles in Ireland signify – just that humans were bonkers, but why should they change?

Would Joanna have had an answer to this?

Walking to the pub in the half dark I was thinking – We must get this over with quickly, and then I can go back to – what? We had had to bring the children with us because we could not leave them in the cottage alone.

In the pub the man unidentifiable as Mr Brewster greeted the children with – 'Hullo me darlings, and what have ye been doing today, except rolling down the hillside curled up inside the tyre of life?' The children looked at him blankly.

I supposed I might explain – That was a game children used to play in mining villages in the nineteen-twenties, when the grown-up life around them was so boring. And that's boring too.

Alix was saying 'How is your leg?'

The man was saying 'As right as a shower of rain.'

And Alix said 'You seemed to be putting it on a bit.'

And the man said 'Ah, it's the food.' Then 'What'll ye be having?'

Alix said 'The children and I would like Cokes, and my husband would like a large whisky and ginger ale.'

Phoebe had wandered off to the bar and seemed to be assessing her chances of getting through to the bottles at the back.

And then the man was saying 'That cottage is a fine old place to have a holiday in.'

Alix was saying 'It's not really big enough.'

The man said 'Ye could do something with the barn. Or the cowshed.'

People in the pub were trying, but not quite succeeding, to pay us no attention. But it was true there was the problem of bringing children into the pub. I felt – But how lucky to live in a place in which such things of no importance can be overlooked.

I had come to Ireland to see if I could find out more about the 'troubles'. But what mattered surely was how life went on in spite of them. The image came into my mind of that picture in Venice – of the woman nursing the child and the man with a spear looking on. And the tempest somewhere far out at sea –

And the girl in the sky indicating it need not affect them?

Alix was already saying to the man in the pub 'I think we must be going'.

The man was saying – 'You will think about it then?'

Alix said 'Yes.'

Then when we were on our way back to the cottage along a now pitch-black lane Alix said 'I didn't mean that I think we shouldn't be leaving this place, I just meant that we should think about it seriously.'

I said 'I know.'

I thought – But what on earth then were you thinking might be serious?

Then a voice came out of the darkness at one side of us – 'Can you help me?'

Alix stopped and said 'Where are you?'

The voice – that of a woman – said 'In the ditch.'

I was thinking – But at that side of the lane there is not a ditch but a hedge. Peter was saying 'Were you riding a bike?' Phoebe was saying 'A bicycle!' The voice said 'Yes.' Peter and I turned and began groping around in front of our feet to our right. Alix held on to Phoebe who was struggling to join us.

I tripped over something and half fell; I thought – I am going over the cliff. I said 'Is that you?' The voice said 'Yes.' I thought – This really is an absurd place! Then – But you're not in the ditch, you're just squatting here. The voice said 'The bicycle's in the ditch.' I said 'Just let me get over you.' Peter said 'I've got it.' The voice said 'Let me help you.' I said 'No I'm all right.' I wanted to say to Alix – No this is not such a bad place!' Phoebe sang 'There was a fine lady rode on a white horse.'

We straightened ourselves out. I thought – And that's that, or not, as the case may be. We trudged along in the dark, the woman coming with us, and Peter pushing the bicycle. I thought – But where was she going? The lane only leads to the cottage and farm buildings. She said 'You're the new people at the cottage.' Alix said 'Yes.' The woman didn't go on to say – And where are you from. I said 'But we're only here for a short holiday.' The woman said 'Oh that's a pity.' Then Peter said 'You've got a flat tyre,' and the woman said 'I never know how to mend a tyre,' and Peter said 'I'll do it for you.' And then the woman said 'Oh thank you, Peter' and I thought – How did she know his name?

Then – But Peter hasn't been stammering!

Then – But she's not like Joanna, no.

The woman left us at the gate to our small front garden. Alix did not ask her in for a cup of tea or anything. The woman said she'd come back in a day or two to see if her bicycle was ready. When she had gone, I said to Peter 'But how did she know your name?' Peter said, still without stammering, 'She was in the Post Office.'

I said 'Oh I see.'

Alix said 'I must go and put Phoebe to bed.'

Peter, watching me, said 'I suppose she wants to get to know you.'

I was thinking – It's when stammerers have something to say of proper importance, that they don't stammer.

I stayed out in the garden; and thought of what I

had intended to be writing.

The point of this was there had been something different about the baby – some awareness – quite apart from any sickness – and Joanna had seen this.

*

The time that I began to see Alix regularly was when Peter was in a pram and there was a conference of neuroscientists in Brighton, which Johnny said he could arrange for me to attend as an observer. This was when Johnny was achieving some prominence in his profession, but was sometimes felt – so far as I understood it – to be encroaching on the risky territories of quantum physics, which in turn was suspected of being more interested in theories than in facts. It was even hinted, though to guard their own interests people did not like to make too much of this, that Johnny was putting a toe into the murky waters of religion.

In Brighton Alix was there with Peter, often on the beach. Much of the talk in the conference hovered above my head like the unseen heavenly objects that they occasionally talked about. It seemed to be accepted that these were unlikely to become more identifiable.

There were two ways, it was suggested by various

lecturers, of setting about trying to understand the workings of the brain: one was to delve anatomically and surgically if necessary within the brain, but with a living subject it would be difficult in this way to conduct the repetitive series of experiments required to acquire any certainty. The other way would be, and was, to construct a computer system outside the brain which would accurately model the functions of the brain, and to conduct experiments upon this. One such system had in fact been built in California which represented one per cent of the human cerebral cortex which contains 1.6 billion neurons with 9 trillion connections between them. (This at least is what I jotted in my notebook: but perhaps my handwriting, as well as my cortex, was becoming fuddled.) If the computer in California, it was added, were to represent the whole human brain, it would occupy the space of several city blocks and use a million watts of electricity and need 6,700 tons of air-conditioning equipment to cool it; and so on. And so on.

The sort of stuff that Johnny and I sometimes talked about was – might there not be a part of each human brain that might be used to some extent to look at what is going on in other parts of the brain; or might not such a faculty, with practice, be encouraged to emerge or even evolve? Such a process might not be able to be tabulated and planned scientifically, because rational speech would be a part of what it was trying and learning to assess. But then – could not something of the sort be learnt by observation of the world outside, and then the light thus gained be used to illuminate the craziness of the outside world, and thus offer the chance of alleviating it. For was it not now claimed scientifically that the observer affected that which was observed? And might not this represent, and be used as, the freedom that humans felt and understood that they had got; but now sometimes seemed to sense they might have lost? That is – a freedom depending on some partnership not with groups of other humans, but with the working of world or universe?

But at this point my brain seemed to float away, fleeing from those computer systems in California; and Johnny would sit with his eyes closed as if he were on the edge of sleep. Then sometimes I would say – Yes I do understand you – And he would say – Steady on!

During breaks in the conference at Brighton I would go out and sit on a bench on the promenade from which I could look out over the beach, and where I might see Alix with Peter in his pram or chair. Or they might be sitting facing each other on the sand. I would sometimes think – And I am that man in the painting keeping an eye on them with his spear.

Johnny would come out and sit with me. He would say 'How are you managing?'

Once, I said 'What's the function of a work of art?'

Johnny said 'Ah, that's it. That's what joins them together.'

'Joins what?'

'The subjective and objective. The inside and outside worlds.'

I was thinking – And what about choice?

Johnny said 'Look, there's Alix and Peter!'

I said 'Yes I know.'

I was thinking – You mean we are free, but in the sense that if we just know that we are free, then things might follow in a way that we would like?

There are for instance those other eyes watching the group from behind the bars of a window.

I remember how Johnny and I went down to join Alix and Peter on the beach. And I was thinking even more wildly – I mean, don't scientists now say that more than ninety per cent of the universe consists of dark energy and dark matter, the nature of which we know nothing about at all, but which we know are there because it is by their existence that the activity of things we do know about can in some way be understood –

I said to Alix 'Peter looks so happy.'

Alix said 'He loves the sea.'

Johnny said 'The other night we had a midnight bathe.'

I said to Peter 'Splash bang wallop.'

Peter was rocking backwards and forwards as if he were in a small boat on the sea.

There was the impression of light coming down and falling on the beach like confetti.

Alix was saying to me 'Are you surviving?'

I was saying 'People play such clever games.'

Alix said 'Then that's all right.'

Johnny said 'I must get back.' Then – 'You don't look directly at the sun, you just know it's there.' Then he set off across the beach towards the conference hotel.

Alix said 'Let's take Peter on to the pier.'

The long pier was like an arm with a fist at the end stretching out into the sea. Boats might bump into the pier, but from the fist people might be saved from drowning.

I said to Peter 'Look, there are seagulls!'

Alix said 'He knows seagulls.'

I said 'Where do they nest, do you know? On ledges in cliffs?'

She said 'Or sometimes a bit further inland, I think.'

4.

I HAD BEEN writing this in Ireland with my table set up in a corner of the walled back garden with the branch of an apple tree hanging over from the untended land outside. My computer was behaving impeccably, but my writing was becoming lost…

My career as a journalist had come to an early cliff-edge in Kenya; how could what had happened to me be described as a 'human interest' story? And anyway, I had undertaken not to talk of it. So I had cobbled up something usual about the dreadful plight of African refugees, which went down quite well. But I would like to have written what might be called a 'superhuman interest story.'

And then after a time I became involved in script-writing for films. I went to Jerusalem to work on a story about the Israeli-Palestinian conflict of the present day. I wrote to Johnny – We are in Schrödinger's Cat territory here: both sides have equally valid contentions about life and/or death, and it is as if we are waiting for a big Hollywood money-man to open the box and look in.

One had somehow to make an audience see – the Palestinians have been here for hundreds of years and now the Israelis are forcibly taking over their homes and land. The Israelis believe that before the Palestinians were heard of this was their home given to them by God, and after the Romans turned them out the rest of the world treated them so abominably that now it can't be imagined how they can have any other home. God does come into it; but still does not seem much help.

But are not humans supposed to sort things out for themselves?

While I was in Jerusalem I used to walk round the Old Town trying to imagine how Jesus might have seen things the last time he came here. The writers of the Gospels implied that he had as it were cursed Jerusalem – for being the place which had killed the prophets and stoned those who had been sent to it by God; he had called the temple a den of thieves, of which one day no stone would be left standing on top of another. So what on earth might humans make of this prognosis now?

But it was not in the Old City that evil now seemed to reside; here were the holy places of three religions functioning and intact – the Christian Church of the Holy Sepulchre, the Muslim Dome of the Rock, and the Wall of the old Temple where Jews still lamented and prayed. It was beyond this enclave in the outskirts of the city that evil seemed to have sprung its trap: here high walls had been built between where new Israeli settlements had intruded, and the makeshift areas where dispossessed Palestinians had taken refuge. These areas, in concentrated miniature, reminded me of the refugee camp in Kenya. In them I used to wander and wonder – should not the whole place perhaps now literally be rendered so that no stone is left standing on another – by some weapon for instance such as Israel's enemies are said to threaten it with? And then something other than possession or sacrifice might be born and rescued from the holy rubble.

High blank walls had rolls of barbed wire leaning over the top of them as if to spy on what might emerge below – to keep people out, to keep people in – the people building the walls thus imprisoning themselves; and the people outside being lost in a maze with no centre nor exit. I thought – But is this not like one of those models of the brain? And would it not need a bomb, or some other such catastrophe, to get it as it were to evolve, to change?

Or could it be by what is called chance?

In the wall of one such alleyway there was a heavy wooden door closed and bolted as if itself were of brick and iron. But then as I passed it opened and a woman appeared from inside holding out to me something at the end of her extended arms that appeared to be either a bundle of old clothes or a baby. I stopped and turned to her. Then almost immediately there appeared behind me in the previously deserted street a posse of men who pushed the woman roughly back through the door and clanged it shut and re-bolted it. I stood quite still, because this seemed the thing to do. The men who were dressed in inconspicuous uniforms came up to me and surrounded me. I looked at them as if I might convey – But I know about this, you see, something like this has happened to me before. Then after a short time they left me. So I wondered – Was that a baby? Should I have taken it? But then the soldiers would have had forcibly to take it back. But anyway, it couldn't have been, it wasn't, a baby: I only thought it might be because –

But then, what is chance?

Or – what would Joanna have done?

It seemed I would have to go back to my hotel and think – no not think, but wait – to see what would happen, what had happened, to let it go on happening. And then whatever had happened would work itself out: would not be without meaning ...

When I got back to my hotel room things seemed slightly out of place as if it might have been searched. Or of course this could be my faulty memory; or the housemaid.

*

I had been writing this in Ireland in my corner of

the walled back garden. I found that every now and then I was coming up against some uncertainty about where on earth I was in time – I was in the garden, all right, but had I not also been at the same time in Jerusalem which I was writing about? But this had been years ago. But was not this one of the things that scientists now wrote about – about time as well as space being a dimension? Within which things could be, were, connected.

I would have liked to talk to Johnny about this. Perhaps I could talk with Peter about the book I had lent him. I had noticed him reading it earnestly in his tent. What would that stuff mean to a younger generation?

Then a voice seemed to come from over the garden wall. 'Excuse me – '

I said 'Yes?

'I hope I'm not disturbing you.' It was the voice of a woman, apparently from the far side of the wall behind me. Or wherever.

I thought – Please do!

When I turned there was the head of a middle-aged woman with grey hair and a black felt hat appearing over the top of the wall. She said 'May I come in for a moment?' I said 'Yes do.'

She began to climb over the wall like a high-jumper in slow motion – head first, then turning upside down when half way over, but here with her behind able to be supported by the bar. I said 'Can I help?' She said 'No absolutely not.' She landed on her feet by my table. I thought – Or she might have been a pole-vaulter. Then – Of course, she's the woman with the bicycle in the ditch.

She said 'I've been wanting to have a word with you.'

I said 'Oh yes.'

'How long are you staying here?'

'Not long. I don't know.'

She said 'It's such a beautiful place. And I'm sure the local people would do anything for you.'

I thought – Really? I said 'It isn't really big enough for us.'

She said 'I'm sure you could take on the barn by the cowshed and make something of it. Or even the cowshed. They're moving out, you know. It's the troubles.' Then she went on quickly because she must have seen I was looking mystified – 'I was talking with Mr Brewster'. And then – 'How many children have you got, just those two that I've met?'

I said 'Yes.' Then – 'One of them's my stepson.'

She said 'Oh yes.'

I was thinking – She might be something to do with Johnny. Or Joanna. Why was I always thinking of Johnny and Joanna. Or perhaps the Care for

Children people. Because of what I had been writing, yes,

Then Peter appeared from the direction of the barn pushing the woman's bicycle. When he was close to us he said without a stammer – 'I've done the tyre.'

She said 'You are an angel. How much do I owe you?'

Peter said 'Nothing.'

They continued to stare at one another as if they were continuing their conversation. I thought – Is this what it will be like if one day we are without words?

The woman said 'Well it's been lovely knowing you all'; and then she left us, pushing her bike and smiling, round the side of the house towards the gate to the lane.

Peter sat down cross-legged on the grass beside me, and it did not seem that he wanted to say anything or to go. Then Alix came out of the back door of the house and crossed the lawn and held out her closed fist upside down towards Peter. She said 'The lady asked me to give you this.' Peter held his cupped hands under Alix's fist, and she seemed to drop something into them. I did not see what it was.

I thought – But when could Alix and the woman have spoken to each other?

Or have I not seen that gesture with the fist before?

Instances in time seemed to be clanging together.

*

The second time I went to Jerusalem on the job of the script for the film was a year or two after the first; and the murderous deadlock between the two sets of inhabitants had expanded, so that it was now Israelis who felt themselves threatened by a possible nuclear missile attack from Iran. This, of course, was denied by the Iranians who insisted, of course, that their admitted nuclear programme was for purely peaceful purposes. However it seemed undeniable that what was happening was that leading scientists in Iran were being assassinated mysteriously by unidentified explosive devices; and so if this was not evidently the work of Israeli secret agents, then what – and so on.

And I was thinking – Well the longer all this uncertainty goes on, the longer I am likely to continue being paid good money for a script that can have no end; and to be kept out of London where the temptations of my relationship with Alix are likely to explode like a bomb.

And this, unlike so much of the stuff going on around me, didn't seem like a lot of old nonsense.

But then one day I had a message from Johnny saying that he wanted to come out and see me, because he had something important and personal to say to me. And of course I thought it might be something to do with me and Alix. We had been seeing more of each other in London while Johnny had been frequently away; we used to go for walks in the Park with Peter in his push-chair; we did not make love nor talk of it, because – because – I think things seemed so good as they were.

And then when Johnny arrived in Jerusalem he was in a strangely preoccupied state, as if he were listening for things, or to things, at some distance from him. We went to a café and drank some local brew of spirits which Johnny seemed to need to calm him or divert him. I had in my pocket my mobile phone (or whatever it was then called). I had been hoping to get a call from Alix in London, who might tell me what Johnny wanted to say. I did not want to miss this call even now when I knew Johnny was coming; at least I would know that Alix had called. But I also thought it better if Johnny did not get to know this when I was with him: or would it be all for the best if he did? But then at times it seemed obvious that he must know what I felt for Alix; and Alix for me? Anyway, I kept my hand on the instrument in my pocket in order to turn it off if it rang when Johnny was with me; but then at least I would know that Alix had called.

However then when Johnny began to talk he was saying things so interesting and unexpected that I felt it important that I should remember his words with some accuracy; so I was tempted to switch the machine in my pocket from its mode of phone to that of recorder; and I hoped that Johnny's voice might be received through the stuff of my pocket. But then I dithered, and ended by leaving the machine just in some way on.

Johnny said – 'You know you and I have in the past sometimes seen things in different ways: I have thought the world might be changed by techniques elucidated by science; you have doubted that the world for humans can be changed much in this way, because human nature will remain the same; and the best that we can do is to make the best of ourselves as we are. Well I'm giving up many of my hopes for science finding answers for humans, even clear answers about the natural world. The more scientists find about the knowable world the more unknowns there appear to be to discover – both at the heart of what are called matter or energy, or at the outer fringes of the universe – and even what scientists have found, they find cannot be pinned down precisely in language or mathematics. This is not to say there's nothing more to be learned; it is just that more will be learned through the enigmas of human experience. You know what they say about dark matter, dark energy; we know that it's everywhere, but we don't know what more to say about it. And that's a good way of beginning to get an understanding of what we might after all be able to do about life, even to change it. Go into it, know what's there, get a feel of it, try it, don't just talk about it. You know this thing they call the God Particle which is supposed to have transformed original energy into matter. Well how the devil can it be a particle that turns energy into particles – where would this original particle have come from? You have to use your imagination, use this sort of energy; use language perhaps to tidy up as far as you can; but plunge in, have a go at it, dance with it. That's energy. And then after that you can look round and ask – what the devil's going on.'

I could feel the instrument in my pocket vibrating. This and the vibrations from what Johnny was saying seemed all so much part of the same – what – thing? energy? matter? – that it did not seem possible to turn anything off. Johnny was watching me. He said 'You can answer if you like.'

I said 'I don't know what I like.'

He said 'Will you look after Alix and Peter?'

I said 'Yes.'

He said 'Thank you.'

I said 'And what will you do?'

He said 'I don't know yet. I'll find out.'

I thought – When he is like this he is like Joanna.

Then – Has he ever met Joanna?

He said 'You answer it.' Then he got up and left.

*

It is here that the time-scale of my story gets unmistakably out of hand: I mean out of the sequence in which things actually happened. This is partly because I, we, became increasingly aware that things that were happening in the present were connected unexpectedly to things that had happened in the past, and might even decisively affect the future if this were recognised; though how indeed were we to know this at the time? One might become aware, yes, that this was how things worked, but hardly how to order them.

And it could be imagined, yes, that this could be something to do with the working of the brain; even perhaps, and more importantly, with some connection between the brain and the outside world. And then oneself might be aware of some sort of influence, as an observer, if still no control, over the outside world.

In Jerusalem I had the time and the solitude to think in more detail about the time I had spent with Joanna and the baby. We had flown to England and taken the baby to the specialist children's hospital that dealt with such cases; we had left it there, and then Joanna and I had left each other. This was what she had planned, required, and I had agreed. It seemed unlikely that we would see each other again. We had not made love; we had scarcely touched. Our so-called 'marriage' seemed non-existent; it was like something that had happened in a film. I did not know why I had agreed to go through with her scheme, except that at the time I wanted to do something dramatic and extravagant that might 'mean' something in the jargon that I used to myself at the time, and might compensate for the impasse that I seemed to have got myself into with Alix. On the one occasion when I had asked Joanna earnestly about her own motivation, she had answered in a style that showed even more of the outlandish force of her nature than I had seen before –

'Look, what the fuck do you think life is – obey the rules, go by the books, and fucking depressing these are too. And then suddenly bang! you see a cloudburst, you see a path to the stars, you are into another dimension. And you either take what is being held out to you, or you don't. But this is the real thing or there is nothing, not even bits and pieces in the void. And this is what you yourself know, or what the fuck are you doing? Are we fucking? Is it ourselves and each other that we love? All right, there was and is always just one great big primordial fuck going on like the one the Holy Ghost had with the Virgin Mary, and that's all. And that's what we're doing, and that's enough for the moment, thank God.'

And soon after this she had gone off on her own. Her parting shot to me being – 'You say you don't believe in miracles?' And then it was as if there was just the passing crack of a bullet going overhead.

*

I spent time in Jerusalem wandering and wondering what Johnny had gone off to do. There were stories about the people that he had previously worked with in America having discovered some so-called 'code' that could be transmitted on the airwaves or internet or whatever and directed to make the software of computers at a distance malfunction; and this in certain large-scale computer-controlled systems could cause a breakdown that might lead to catastrophic explosion. I understood little of the technicalities of this, but I wondered if this was the sort of weapon that it was feared that Iran or some neighbouring country might develop to use against Israel; or indeed that Israel might develop to defend itself by threatening a pre-emptive strike. But then if some such 'code' could be sent on airwaves then what might be the power of the projection of human thought – was not this the sort of question that Johnny had been asking? And how on earth might it one day be answered?

Johnny had had a story that nowadays when there was a science programme on television the presenter liked to have one or two celebrities in the studio-audience who could be asked to come down on to the stage and the occasion be treated as stand-up comedy. One well-known comic was greeted by the presenter with – 'Oh here you are!' to which the comic replied 'Or am I not also at the other end of the universe?' Which was supposed to, and probably did, put the audience at their ease, because it would show they were acquainted with quantum physics.

And then one night in Jerusalem I had a dream. I was sitting on a beach with my back to the sea and Johnny was in front of me where the sand ended, and he was giving a lecture. To illustrate what he was saying he was using as a blackboard the fence at the back of the beach which was made of vertical slats of wood, this making his diagrams and letters and figures somewhat broken and disjointed. Near the top of this blackboard he had made a simple line-drawing of what seemed to be a large bird gliding towards the audience with down-turned wings; or perhaps it was a man on a tightrope with his long balancing-pole weighed down at each end by gravity. Johnny was on the left of the blackboard area, moving to and fro in front of his illustrations as lecturers do. He was trying to add something to what seemed to be a complex formula at the extreme right tip of the bird's wing, or the tightrope-walker's pole, but there seemed to be not enough room at the fence's edge; his chalk kept on slipping off into the air. And then I, from the beach, raised a hand and asked a question – 'Are you trying to write a formula for what humans don't yet know?' And Johnny turned and looked at me; and then there was a flash where his hand had gone off the end of the blackboard, and all his illustrations and writing disappeared. And then there was nothing. I suppose just the beach and the sea. But I was remembering what there also had been.

*

I was remembering this dream when I was writing some years later in Ireland, and I wondered – but what are humans doing about what they don't know now?

I had wondered if Peter wanted to talk to me about the book I had lent him; also perhaps if I should be asking him about his stammer. I did not know if it was right for him to be cut off in Ireland from any professional help. So I thought that the next day I would ask him to come with me to help with some shopping in the small harbour-town by the sea; and then we would have time and space to talk.

So off we went side by side in my small family car, and then what had seemed right suddenly seemed wrong. I remembered being told by someone who seemed to know that a stammer at Peter's age disappears quickest if it is left alone and not talked about; talking only buttons it up as if in a strait jacket. And indeed the book on modern physics and ancient Eastern mysticism surely implied much the same; talk usually calcifies and solidifies the past; it is what happens that is free and builds the future.

In the town there was almost no one in the main street by the harbour. I wondered if this was because of rumours of the re-emergence of the so-called troubles. And then had there not been the goings-on about the whale washed up on the smugglers' beach? But these had seemed ridiculous. Now there was just one old woman on the road hobbling with a stick and pushing a large shopping basket on wheels in front of her. But then a large dog appeared and seemed to be attacking and trying to get at whatever was in her basket. I had been saying to Peter 'Was there anything your mother wanted you to get?' and Peter had stammered and then had shaken his head. A man appeared from a door of a house at the side of the street and had what appeared to be a shot-gun on a strap over his shoulder. I thought – But that is not Mr Brewster: or is Mr Brewster just the generic name for all the men and their strange behaviour in this neighbourhood. The man was taking whatever it was down from his shoulder; the old woman was swinging at the dog with her stick. I had been parking the car at the kerb. Peter leaned out of his window and shouted loudly 'Leave the dog alone!' The dog turned to look at Peter: the old woman managed to give it a whack with her stick: the man disappeared quickly back into his house. Peter scrambled out of the car and ran towards the dog. I did nothing. Peter had stopped by the dog and held out his hand to it and the dog sniffed it. Then what sounded like an alarm bell began ringing somewhere behind me. I wondered – Could that have been set off by some Mr Brewster? Peter was coming back to the car holding the dog by the scruff of its neck. He said fluently 'Have we got anything for it to eat at home?' I said 'I'm sure we can find something.' I turned to look at the old lady but she was trundling quickly round a corner out of sight. The alarm bell stopped ringing. Peter had opened the rear door of the car and was gesturing for the dog to get in. The dog looked up at me as if politely. I nodded. The dog clambered in. When we were driving up the hill away from the town I said to Peter 'Well that worked well.' I thought – One doesn't stammer at moments of importance? And then things work out themselves?

*

The next day I was trying to make up my mind whether or not we should leave Ireland because of the uncertainties of the situation, or whether we should settle down here for a while, where Peter and Phoebe seemed able to feel so free and so much at home. I could hear them now downstairs playing with the dog, which they seemed intent on keeping. I thought of putting a notice about ownership in the post-office window, but the people in the farm buildings said it was known to be a stray.

Peter saw me watching them with the dog from the top of the stairs. He said 'Are we in the way?' I said 'What are you going to call her?' Phoebe said 'Smelly.' I said 'Why'. Phoebe said 'Because she sniffs me.' I said 'That's because she's fond of you.' Phoebe said 'I know.' Peter said 'I've been reading that book you lent me.' I said 'Oh yes'. Peter said 'It seems to be saying we can make our own reality if we pay attention to what's around us.' I said 'Well I suppose then something becomes our reality which it might not have had a reason to do otherwise.'

*

I was finding it difficult to go on writing about my time in Jerusalem because things kept on butting in as if to tell me I should be paying more attention to the present; or perhaps, all right, to connections between the present and what had been happening during my time in Jerusalem. I had thought before – Either things seem to be happening all at once, or nothing of any significance seems to be happening at all. So indeed – Why not try to write it like that? But in life – How might one try to deal with it like that?

I was still trying to make up my mind about leaving Ireland. The short lease on our cottage was nearly up. Things kept cropping up to suggest that we might extend both the lease and even the living accommodation. What did this mean? I thought I should go for yet another walk to the top of the cliff to empty my head and see if anything further came in.

Then when I was there, I thought I should go down to the beach and see if there was anything left of the whale that had been washed up. I had once imagined jumping over the cliff, had I not. And seeing if I could bounce on the whale. I must have been thinking of Joanna's style. There was a steep path down the cliff-face which did not look now much more inviting than the jump. What did mystics have in mind when they said that one should not assess the fruits of any action, but only attend to the care of the seeds? This was what Joanna had been on about? Why was I suddenly thinking so much of Joanna! Well, why not.

I slipped and slithered the last few yards to the beach. There were no marks on the sand; had the whale existed? But of course the tide had come in and gone out several times in linear time, under the tug of the moon. Had I not once thought what a wonderful place the beach would be to play games on? There had not been enough of us? Or we were too busy? And now there were no humans in sight.

But there was that dog Smelly, who seemed to have followed me and was watching me from the top of the cliff. It had its head on one side as usual, as if asking me – You're not really thinking of going, are you, now that you've only just got me; and we could all play games on the beach? I then thought – And hadn't I thought it might be a dog that that girl was watching from behind her bars in the sky?

Or suddenly now – that sort-of baby in Jerusalem?

I thought I should hurry home and tell Alix that I now thought – and she had already shown that she would agree, hadn't she? – that we shouldn't be leaving.

5.

But now, could I write about what had happened in Jerusalem?

My script-writing job had come up against a blank wall like one of those constructed in the suburbs of the city. I would go to the café in which Johnny and I had sat and try to get my mind off on a viable tack. If it was evident that these walls should come down, then would not a suitable means be a weapon like the one on which Johnny had apparently worked in California – something transmitted on the airwaves and demolishing things at a distance. But this only blew up stuff run by other computers, not walls. Walls were in people's minds, yes, but not in the style in which they could be blown up by computers. Not even in the minds of the people who might use such devices, who thought their minds were computers. This was getting confusing. Or might there be a way of experimenting with, influencing people's minds, without taking them out and fiddling with them or building a cooling system as big as Chicago –

Was this what Johnny had been working on?

Anyway, just blowing up people who were like walls was no use. This had been tried for years, and left not even roads or pathways.

And what could be shown in a film, except ever more blatant apocalypses. In the book I had given to Peter it seemed to say – Just carry possibilities in your mind, and then things are done for you.

Oh well, let Peter's generation get on with it.

But at the same time was I not finding life nowadays too difficult – sitting in the café in which Johnny and I had sat and drinking a somewhat stupefying brew of beer, and dreaming about the chances of one day being able to get messages (thought messages!) to or from Alix on the airwaves. I had not been able to get in touch with her since Johnny had come and gone a few days ago. Perhaps she did not know what to say, as indeed I did not, as well as not knowing what was happening. But I was still under contract to the film people. And what exactly had Johnny meant when he had asked me – Would I look after Alix and Peter? And I had said emphatically just – Yes. So had not that been fixed. And was it not now proper to wait and see what would happen?

I was in the café and looking out through the plate-glass window at the street and was thinking – Am I not now like the girl at that barred window in the sky? And then – What on earth was she looking at – a dog, or something more heavenly?

And then a young girl, a child, came into the café, and went first to a man at the next table and held out her hand to him; and then seemed to have made a mistake, and came to my table and held out her hand to me. But not, no, with fist clenched and upside down (I am you see writing this now): so I thought she must be a beggar. But then she turned and dashed quickly out of the café. And then a bomb went off in the street outside.

I had just enough time perhaps to think – So someone has got the code, have they? But of what; and is this right?

But there was no time to think of anything else. And for how long I do not know.

I had been sitting close to the window, so the glass from the blast cut me about the head and face. When I woke I thought I had been blinded, and hoped to become unconscious again, or even dead, so that I should not know this. But about what had I been thinking just before? Joanna? The child? What had happened to the child? How old would it be now?

I became somewhat more conscious in the ambulance on my way to hospital. I was aware that my face was bandaged, so I might not be blind: I had probably been sedated. Perhaps I was on my way to the Horn of Africa, where I had been tossed like a bullfighter? There was not much pain. Did Joanna feel pain? Or was it Alix who knew pain but also knew where things were going. I must have been unconscious during and after my arrival in hospital, for when I became aware again it was of someone sitting by my bed. I managed to open one eye. I said – 'Alix?'

She said 'You're awake!'

I said 'What are you doing here?'

She said 'You knew I'd be here!'

I thought – Did I? Then – But I thought I was going to go and look after you, not you come and look after me.

She was saying 'What's the difference?'

*

It was in the hospital that my story abandoned its track in linear time, and looked around half blindly for meaning. Or rather, looked back on this time in hospital; for isn't it the task of writing to look for meaning? This was in spite of the fact that Johnny and I had kept on saying that so-called 'meaning' could not be put into words. But could not a spot-light be shone on it by words, as if in an underground cavern?

Also, yes, I was now finding myself trying to pick out other people's representations, as well as my own.

The story that I picked up from Alix during my time in hospital was that Johnny had been round to my flat in London to see if there were any messages for me which he could send on to me. But then when he heard I had been injured, he and Alix agreed that she should fly out to be with me, and he had said that he had even mentioned something about this to me. And in the meantime he would take care of whatever the messages had been about. It was at this point that Alix's and my flashlights seemed inevitably to be lighting up possibly varying images; but we neither of us imagined that either of us were not being honest. Is it not thus that history anyway gropes along? With the best chances of bringing back to life what actually happened.

I gathered that there had been one message at my flat which was something to do with Joanna. Alix said – No, Johnny at that time would not have known who Joanna was, and in hospital of course it was you who were thinking of Joanna. I would say – No, I was thinking of you. And Alix would say – Of course. But then later I would be thinking – Well Johnny would still have good reasons not to tell Alix about Joanna: though he wanted Alix and I to look after each other. And of course Peter.

And then years later the stuff that I was writing about did seem to be happening in the way I was writing it, though closer to the time in which I was writing than to the time I was writing about. But then isn't this to do with what scientists say about the nature of time?

Johnny of course had been aware of the makeshift nature of his and Alix's marriage; he also must have been aware of my and Alix's affinity with one another. I do not know, or cannot remember, how much he had gleaned about my experience with Joanna; but at moments when we were both drinking I had doubtless released into the air something about my past or present at the time when he was first seeing Alix and getting her pregnant. Oh things had happened that were both wrong and right! But would sort themselves out if we did not turn our backs. We would see. But I had undertaken not to talk about it. So – so what. Of course Johnny's interest had been stirred about whoever might be Joanna. It would not have been only I who felt that there might be, should be, some transposition not only in our own relationships, but from the social and moral order in which no learning was accepted except that of rules. In morals there was some fluidity; but this was treated like the dripping of a tap.

It had struck me, of course, how alike in some ways Johnny and Joanna were in style and temperament: one did things on what seemed demand; then took responsibility for what you had done. Whereas Alix and I seemed to go with what happened.

But might all this fit if we were all together?

*

In the years in which in spite of demands and acceptance nothing much seemed to be happening, Johnny was away for a time in California, then briefly in Geneva playing a small part in the Large Hadron Collider's search for the particle that was supposed to be the link between the energy of the original Big Bang and the emergence of matter in the form of stars and planets of the universe. But, as Johnny so frequently said – How on earth do you justify trying to find what transforms energy into particles by looking for a particle?' I said 'By spending endless years in a very well-paid job in Geneva.' Johnny said 'Rather like your films.' Then – 'Well I'm off, anyway.'

I continued, yes, to go to and fro between London and Jerusalem – perhaps this was how my memory became ambivalent about exactly when the bomb went off. But in my work there was no ambiguity about big money being made by stories of tragedy and apocalypse or farce. I would ruminate – Because anything else is felt to be boring if believable?

In London Alix looked after the flat and then a small house; Peter went to and from school, and sometimes in the holidays to spend weekends or perhaps a week with his father. After a time Phoebe was born, from the beginning as if with a wand in her hand. Eventually I quarrelled with the film people because they changed my script so much in order not to offend anyone but me; so I walked out, and the film flopped at the box office, which made me feel both justification and regret. So I turned my attention to writing about politics, where of course people still fiddled with the real world, but made no attempt to call it art.

The last time I went to Jerusalem I was to be televised talking at some of the locations in the film; and this did coincide, yes, with Johnny being on one of his visits to England to spend time with Peter. And here and now he did, yes, pick up a message for me and showed it to Alix and they opened it; and they said that they did try to get hold of me, but I was said to be unavailable. So then Alex said 'He always said he'd promised her not to get involved any further.' And Johnny said 'And he always told me that she and I would get on like a house on fire.' And so Alix agreed. She was always very practical.

The message, which I saw as soon as I got home, was from the Care for Children people, and asked if I had any news of someone who had once worked for them whom they had known only as Joanna. She had been back in Kenya making enquiries with them, and then was said to have been trying to get into Somalia, for what purpose was not known. It was feared she might have been abducted by pirates.

I said 'This was something I was imagining happening. Years ago when I thought I was blind after the bomb had gone off.'

Alix said 'Perhaps it did.'

I said 'What?'

She said 'Nothing.'

'You mean there might have been a message like this then? This is an old message? I mean, it might be a fake? A story?'

'You're better leaving it to Johnny.'

'Why.'

'He wants to become involved in something like this.'

'And I'm looking after Peter and Phoebe and you.'

'Yes.'

This must have been before we got a second message, when we were back in Ireland after a short break in London, which said that it seemed that the person I had known as Joanna had been trying to get into Kenya via Somalia; but my informant, who did not want to give me his or her name for security reasons, assured me that everything possible was being done at his or her end, and so I was not to worry.

I said to Alix 'It's a wonder how anyone dealing in international affairs ever imagines they know anything of anything going on at all.'

Alix said 'I don't think they do, do they?'

The story that we later got from Johnny was that he had found out what he could from the Care for

Children people, which was not much. Perhaps they thought he was a reporter who would jeopardise any negotiations in which they might become involved concerning whatever it was that Joanna might be involved in; the details of which they did not yet know, no. And so yes, all right, this was at least a good excuse for doing nothing. And in Ireland we could get on with wondering about the chances of it being right that there seemed nothing we could do.

I think Johnny at this time – and Joanna before him – had got fed up with the feeling that life was useless whether or not it could be said that clear and rational decisions had effect. Or if life were paradoxical, then what? Lay down and die? Or did this lead to – come bursting out of a tomb –

Peter, or was it Alix, once said to me during this time – 'Then did you mean that this was some sort of Biblical story?'

I thought – Yes. No. Yes. No. Yes.

Johnny had used to say 'But what about you?'

I had said 'I was carried along by her.'

'And then it stopped?'

I had said 'I don't think it's stopped.'

So Johnny went off to look for Joanna.

He travelled from Yemen, across the sea to the Horn of Africa. I mean this is the story he told to people who questioned him. It is quite possible, he used to say, that he was followed or watched, because he was a recognised scientist after all and was travelling for what reason in such areas? (Afterwards Johnny would say – 'Oh yes, wasn't I famous enough? Or not famous enough. Whichever fits in.') He bought or hired a small sailing boat in Aden (was it?) and how much did he know about sailing, all right, or indeed know or even think if he was going in the right direction. But isn't this the point? Unequivocally alone, you are out of the benumbing human world of either-ors, this-or-thats: things happen, you feel required, and you respond. Well why do men and women sail across what are to them uncharted seas; tread alertly into jungles; travel across ice-caps to unmarked poles? The only either-or worth putting to the test of such experiences is – either there is a God with you or there is not. But if there is not, then doesn't that mean that there's nothing but yourself? And so you can act God?

Johnny would say only 'I remember the fish, and of course the clouds. And one has to watch out not to be knocked into the sea by the boom.

– Is that why it is called a boom?'

He landed somewhere on the coast of Somalia. (I am talking in place of Johnny here because he says he can't or won't talk about it. I know, or remember, what he means about this: when you have given up intention, will, and have handed it elsewhere entirely, you do not want to go back over it or it may break; your footsteps may break it like fragile glass; for this is what it seems like after all, if you are in the air and over an abyss.) Local people turned up to seize his boat. They seized Johnny. He behaved as if this was what he had expected, even had come for. He wanted to see how things would work out; well this is what you do as a scientist, isn't it? He said this to them. Did it matter if no one understood him? He was hoping to find a woman, a woman of his dreams, well this was what men did, wasn't it? Or hadn't they come across this yet? But he was hoping to come across people who might know about her – this with a big smile. They roughed him up a little; saw if he would bounce. These were his words. I had been thinking – You had in a way wanted to die? He had once said – Well we all sometimes do, or should do, don't we? And both then and now – I've said this was a scientific experiment.

They pulled his boat up into the sand dunes and turned it over and tried to hide it by covering it with sand.

Then they tied his hands, and half pulled him half pushed him a mile or two inland.

And in the meantime, what had he been able to find out about Joanna?

Joanna was someone as if always alone in a boat on storm-tossed seas. Did she feel she acted God? Well how much do people know about God. There were stories she had lived in Mexico, she had lived in Cuba: well of course there were times when she wanted to die. She would say with a blatantly false smile – I don't betray my sources. I sometimes think that Johnny might have known her during these years. But one doesn't, no, betray one's sources.

Johnny always insisted that his captors had not treated him badly. (He used to put it – If you want peace on earth, then behave as if there is peace on earth.) The way in which his captors treated him might or might not have had something to do with their assumption that he might or might not have been an agent sent to spy on them (but as an enemy? A friend?) Both sides keep their cards close to their chests. With or without God looking over their shoulder.

The story that Johnny seemed unequivocally keen to tell at this time and for everyone to remember (and not only perhaps because it was a good story?) was –

At the headquarters of the gang of tribesmen who had taken him prisoner he had been placed with a guard in a rather large tent that must have been looted from one of the refugee camps in the area. There, to pass the time, he occupied himself by drawing with his finger on the sand how much he could remember of the complex code – a lengthy series of noughts and ones and letters – which was used in the device which, by transmission on the airwaves, could be used to cause malfunction in computers a thousand miles away, and thus cause explosions in appropriate systems. This code was something he had been shown and had tried to memorise in California. He had not got very far with it then; and in the tent in the wasteland he doubted if he was getting anywhere at all. But he had never liked the idea of transmission on such airwaves anyway; and had made comments, teasingly or not as the case might be, about why not transmission by thought-waves if one was thinking of transmission on the air at all. Or at least an experiment or two; might not that do the trick? And now in the tent he saw his guard watching him intently – well, yes, exactly. So when he had marked out on the sand what seemed to him a sizeable array of letters and signs and gobbledegook, he sat crossed-legged in front of it and closed his eyes and waved his hands above what might be, indeed, yes, in whatever sense, some charm of magic symbols. He thought of humming a tune: but no, not hum. Why not pray? Surely, in the circumstances. So he prayed.

(I can't believe no one ever asked him – What exactly did you say? But I did not.)

Anyway Joanna had gone back in the meantime to the refugee camp in Kenya to see if she could find out more about the ancestry of the child she had taken to the specialist hospital in London years ago. At that time (so we all learned later) the doctors had insisted on keeping the child for further observation and tests, because in the course of treatment for water-on-the-brain they had observed other abnormalities in the child's cerebral formation; about which they did not want to offer any further opinion yet, because the brain and indeed the baby itself, after what they had been through, should have a chance to rest and settle down. So it was agreed with Joanna – with whom it seemed to suit everyone concerned to agree she was the person to deal – that the baby should remain in the care of the hospital until a time when further tests and observations could be made and assessed. Until then, Joanna was assured, the baby would be treated with the utmost care and attention because – because – well, so far as they could tell at the moment it was evidently a special and potentially most interesting case. And for this reason, in order that other would-be interested parties should not come blundering in, could Joanna please be sure not to mention to anyone the possibility of the baby being out of the ordinary; to which Joanna replied with a convincing nod of the head.

And thus for a time the situation concerning the baby had remained, and Joanna went on her way. It seemed also crucial for her not to talk about what might, goodness knows, be seen as her own special case; which was, as will have been gathered, to seem to carry within her an awareness of certain tasks and obligations from which she would allow no deviation, and to which others seemed to yield even if they did not understand. So Joanna remained a haunted and haunting Sphinx-like figure in various oases in their deserts, until some further impulse seemed to be wafted to her in a gust of sand – that she should after all try to find out more about the ancestry of the baby.

This at least was Johnny's way of putting it.

And indeed Johnny had come to notice that some of the band of men who were holding him prisoner were now gathering to watch him as he sat in his tent with closed eyes presiding over his mantras in the sand. And the number of watchers grew; and then the head man with his entourage appeared, in front of whom Johnny had been arraigned when he had arrived. And they all watched while Johnny swayed slightly above his magic signs and numbers – well what do people think they are doing when they pray? And if on the airwaves you can blow up installations a thousand miles away – well, you can imagine this sort of process if not talk about it much. And sometimes the watchers whispered amongst themselves. And then Johnny thought – Well this is the sort of thing I have wanted to do experiments about, is it not, call it what you will. And then he might have turned and smiled at his audience, because he saw them recoil. And so he thought – All right, the result of this experiment may be that you think I am threatening you with a curse.

This at least was the way in which Johnny's story hung in the air, if not always exactly as he told it. But after a time what his captors seemed to be murmuring about was in what manner to release him – for they did not want to bring any further threat of black magic down on themselves, did they. Though in later years Johnny would often end his story – All right, they had got all they could out of me and just wanted an excuse to be rid of me. Will that do?

And in the meantime the time had long since come in the hospital in London when it had become evident that the baby was now too old to be accommodated suitably in a public ward; so the baby was transferred to a Carc for Childrcn home for those who were waiting for adoption. But the hospital authorities still insisted that they needed to be carrying out observation and tests on the baby and her brain or 'mind' as one might call it as she developed – she was now old enough to be known as 'she,' and her brain after all was part of her whole body and her environment. But still, for scientific discipline and incorruptibility, please would no one still say too much about her.

One of the occasional mysteries of this time was how Johnny, with his special interest in neurology, had not heard of her: but then indeed perhaps he had – even possibly during my second time in Jerusalem when the bomb had gone off. And then might he not have had his own particular reasons for not talking about it? How on earth do historians ever think they have wholly untangled history! Are there not always sound reasons, as well as odd ones, for keeping things concealed? Anyway – Johnny had gone off to learn more from his neuroscientists; and the child had played apparently happily in a well-run nursery home.

But then the time inevitably came when those who had made themselves responsible for watching and studying the development of the child said – But she needs to be in some sort of recognisable family environment, in order that what has been and is being observed as special about her may have a chance to grow and develop naturally, and not be swamped because she is seen as an oddity. It is accepted, is it not, that the seeds of a change, of a step in evolution, come about by a chance – whatever chance may be – in the make-up of a cell or gene or a group of cells or genes; but whether this unscheduled (as it were) development lives or dies, propagates or withers, depends on the nature of the environment in which it finds itself. This can be observed of course in plants, and supposedly in animals; and so, it can be conjectured, it might be observed in humans. The rogue gene falls from who knows where; but it is in accordance with the family or other relationships it finds itself with that it flourishes or fails; and this can not only be studied but might be assisted or reproduced. This girl is growing too fast and too uniquely for even the best nursery school to be the sort of place required for her. We are in fact making efforts to find what might be a warm but wise family home.

This was at roughly the same time that Joanna got the idea of trying to trace any signs of what might be found of the girl's actual family. During Joanna's intimacy with her dying mother she had learned something of the mother's parentage. To try to follow up in practice such an impulse now might seem crazy in the flux and chaos of the population of East Africa; also, was not the peculiarity of the girl that she was a changeling from her ancestry, so how would it help to re-establish contact with her forebears? But as Johnny put it to us later – That sort of common-sense reasoning did not mean much to Joanna. In fact, it should not carry much weight with anyone who has followed the story so far. The background to this story is that of a common-sense world in which the human rationale is to get power over others by manipulating them or if necessary by bashing them to bits. What one may hope to find within all this is a seed that will have some contact with another kind of world – call it another dimension, as scientists do, or what you will – but one in which you do not follow common sense, but seem to respond to somc command from outside you.

And if at this point someone would say to Johnny – Well, but after all, with Joanna, where did it in fact lead? Johnny would say simply – to me.

Anyway, Joanna set off on her determined wild-goose chase because – because no one found themselves keen to ask her why. She is remembered as returning to the refugee camp in Kenya and making enquiries at the bungalow of the Care for Children people, but they paid little attention to her and gave her what seemed little help. Their minds seemed to be occupied with the story of a plane-crash that had taken place in the wilderness just over the border with Somalia, and from which there was said to be just one survivor – a man, who was rumoured to be some secret service or double agent, for what had happened to the other people in the plane? They had been taken by local tribesmen, the so-called 'pirates'; and just this man left to be rescued? This story made no sense, but then no one need be doing anything about it. Joanna had a fantasy that the single survivor might be myself – the writer of this story – well, was I not the man who had turned up out of the blue all those years ago to help her have the baby; and would not this fit in with the sort of style that she trusted? That is – might not such a seemingly miraculous occurrence be a concomitant to what was at issue with the brain? Joanna had presumably hardly thought about me for years; but she found someone among the Care for Children people who thought she knew the location of what was said to be the crashed plane. But then Joanna was told – The plane doesn't exist, the story's a cover-up, a blind, we've been told to say no more about it. Then from someone she had known in the camp before, she heard – Yes, that's an old crash, don't you remember it, just over the border, it's been there for years. So what if it's a cover-up. Joanna said – Can you show me exactly where it is on the map? And the woman said – I'll drive you as far as the border if you like, but don't tell anyone.

And in the meantime it was being indicated to Johnny by his captors that he was to be released, so he need not draw any more magic spells or curses in the sand. Johnny indicated, no doubt unintelligibly, that he had no idea where he was, and so could they possibly – . He stared at them and they stared back at him. It probably occurred to them that he might not have quite finished with his curses. He had told them when they had come across him, though he had not known if they had understood him, that he was looking for a certain lady. They now nodded vigorously. These gestures made him wonder if they might somehow have some knowledge of Joanna. He was, of course, hungry and thirsty and somewhat disorientated.

There was one truck in the tribal compound which it seemed to be the prerogative of the head man to use, with a man who struggled to be an interpreter as driver. Johnny was heaved up carefully and placed in this truck. He used to say that he did now seriously try to transmit thought from his head – to Joanna, for instance, who he had been trying to find and now needed to find him. He would say later that this was an interesting experiment, because it did seem to help him not only to maintain his façade as an influential guru or ju-ju man, but because being fastened horizontally on the floor of the truck it helped alleviate pain in his back. He says he also tried to transmit a thought-message to me, the writer of this story, on the lines of – There might be evidence for the existence of thought messages if the experiment is done in extreme physical and psychological uncertainty: after all, what one is talking about is some way of getting to the end of one's tether.

The truck had come to what seemed to be the wrecked fuselage of an aeroplane that had crashed or made a forced landing in the scrub-land some time ago. To Johnny it seemed that this might be, or might have been, some response to his thought-efforts; of course this would be nothing following logically, except that his abductors did indeed seem to be going to release him here anyway. One wing of the plane had been removed altogether, and the fuselage had been broken into along its entire length and evidently looted. Johnny's captors freed him and gestured that he should get out of the truck and into the hollow of the fuselage; they mimed him lying down comfortably in the shade. Johnny smiled and mimed as if he were grateful to them. He thought – Well at least they are not killing me. He clambered up into the plane. Then – Well at least now I can choose how to live or die. But then after all – Choosing how to live or die may not be so easy.

Joanna had been having such conversations with herself for years. But now, trudging through scrub-land having been dropped off from her friend's truck, she was finding herself in a situation in which she was missing the companionship of her baby. This was the landscape in which it had all begun; of course she had felt herself incapable of providing an environment for the baby then: but now – how old would it be: and how old would be the man who had done so much for her: and did she really think it was he who she was looking for now? In an aeroplane that had crashed: oh yes very suitable, very symbolic. What was that friend of his he once talked about, that one who was studying the processes of the brain? Oh well, does this all mean that this is what I now should be doing, yes. But I don't want to die, no. I don't want anyone to find my dead body in the body of a plane.

She was moving in the direction in which her friend with the truck had pointed. Her friend had said – But you are mad, there's no one there, it's all in your mind. She had thought – Yes this is all in my mind. Her friend had said – Look, you can have my mobile phone, you can call me, you know how to work a mobile phone? She had said – No. Her friend had said – Bloody hell, then you're on your own. Joanna had thought – Yes No Yes. Her friend had said – Anyway here it is, take it.

When she was walking she was thinking – What I really want to do is lie down and look at the sand just in front of my eyes, the billions and billions of grains of it like the suns and stars. Then there was something in front of her shaped and curved like a chute or the start of another dimension. She thought – Yes that is what I have been looking for. She walked towards it.

Then she thought – How lucky I brought a bottle of water with me!

Johnny was lying in the hollow fuselage of the

plane when Joanna's head appeared just beyond his feet. He said 'Hullo, who are you?' Then – 'I know you!' She said 'You're not who I thought you were, but I expect I know you.' Then he said 'And is that water?' She said 'Yes.' He thought – The dry land can wait. While he drank, she crawled into his arms and slept.

6.

I HAD BEEN writing in my small upstairs room in Ireland. I had talked with Alix, and we had decided not to leave the cottage. I had thought – What, at the instigation of a stray dog? And then – No or yes, what's the difference.

Peter was waiting under the open flap of his tent in the garden. He said 'You were going to tell me what's the difference between a Biblical story and a real-life story.'

I thought – Oh haven't we done that? I said 'Oh yes, well, we never really know enough of what might make a real-life story true – there are so many different views, interpretations, events and influences behind the scenes that no one knows anything about. A Biblical story tries to put before you something you can feel you have experience of being true, however much it may not conform to usual ways of seeing, things as true.'

Peter said 'You mean it's true on another level.'

I said 'Yes, perhaps the only level on which there's much sense in the word.'

I was thinking – Well how should, how did, the story I am writing continue? They are asleep in one another's arms in Africa. Well we know this part of the story is true. About the crashed plane, the 'pirates,' there are so many stories that hardly anyone begins to think of any of them as true.

Peter said 'Then how do we know what to do?'

I said 'By what has happened to us being true.'

Peter began to say something, stopped; but was not stammering. He smiled at me and moved away.

I was thinking – But it is what happens to and with the girl that should be true – concerning what is both around her and within her.

But how do the couple I've got so assuredly in the fuselage of a crashed plane get out? Oh yes, they've been given a mobile phone. Johnny will know how to work it. They hear the sound of a helicopter overhead –

– But the child is all this time in London. Why did they have to go all the way to Africa?

Well they had to meet somewhere, didn't they?

Peter came wandering back. He said 'That lady with the bike's been here again.'

I said 'Oh yes, what's she been on about?'

'She was talking with the people who are doing up the barn and the cowshed.'

'Oh yes, but you know about that, don't you.'

'I know we may not be leaving. But why can't we talk about it.'

'People may not like it.'

'You mean the troubles.'

'Oh yes the troubles.'

Peter said 'Well I like it.' Then with a smile again, just as he was turning away – 'They seemed to like the money.'

Phoebe came running out of the house. She seemed more grown up nowadays, as if waiting to take on responsibility. I quite often found myself wondering what the girl we had tried to rescue would be looking like now; she would be more Peter's age than Phoebe's.

Phoebe was saying 'Mummy says can you come and talk to her. She's in the kitchen. There's been an accident at the airport.'

I thought – An accident at the airport?

Peter said 'It wasn't a crash. I think it's just a hold-up.'

'What do you know about it?'

'The lady was talking about it.'

'In the cowshed?'

'With Mr Brewster. She was just saying they'll be later than they thought.'

'Who. Yes of course. I know who. Wait here.'

As I was going into the house Peter said 'I thought one of them might be my father.' I was thinking – You shouldn't believe everything you hear. Then – Yes of course you should believe it if you think it's true. Then – Oh stop twittering.

I found Alix in the kitchen, sitting quietly with

her hands in her lap. I said 'That lady's here?'

Alix said 'She wants to know what we've heard about Johnny.'

'What has she heard.'

'There's talk about him having been on some secret work for the government, so that's why it's being hushed up. But of course that's nonsense. I mean that's why we can say it's being hushed up. I mean we needn't worry if they're late.'

'Why did she come to you?'

'Well I'm supposed to be married to him I suppose.'

I said 'I would have said you're married to me.'

She said 'Of course.'

I said 'We know what work he was doing.'

She said 'Of course.'

There were lights flashing on and off in my head, as if to signal the arrival of a lift or an imminent explosion. I said 'He was looking for Joanna. How much did he tell you about all that.'

'About as much as you told me.'

'I mean about me and Joanna.'

'Same answer.'

'Oh all right.' I thought – Of course cover-ups are all right, so long as you are aware there is truth.

Alix said 'They were thinking about the baby.'

I said 'Did Johnny tell you about all that?'

The lift seemed to have arrived. Or perhaps it had

stopped at the floor below, and we would all pile into nothingness.

Then Alix said 'All right, why didn't you and Joanna keep it?'

I thought of saying – She didn't want to. Then I said 'It had to have specialist treatment.'

Alix said 'Doesn't it still have to have specialist treatment?'

I said 'Of a different kind.' Then – 'Now is the time to keep it.'

Alix said 'I know.'

I thought – Now is the time to press an emergency button: that is, if there were an emergency.

I said 'Will you do that?'

Alix said 'Of course.' Then – 'I'm your wife, aren't I?'

I said 'Yes.' I thought – And of course, yes, the grey-haired lady must have known all about this, but what will she be able to do about the rest of the world.

*

Into a room which looked like one that might be used by a judicial committee was ushered the grey-haired lady whose style of wearing a long black coat and a black peaked cap made her sometimes look like a military commander. The other occupants of the room were four men and three women, who sat in a row at the far side of a long table. A comfortable chair had been placed for the grey-haired lady facing the table. She nodded with a smile at two or three of the people opposite her, and they nodded back. Then the man at the centre of the row said 'I understand this meeting is to be strictly informal and confidential, and no minutes are to be taken. Is that correct?' The grey-haired lady said 'Yes.'

The man said 'I have passed the one copy of your statement between the eight of us, and they have read it. I understand you did not want more copies made, and you want this copy back.'

The lady said 'That is correct.'

'Can we first just understand, and so get it out of the way, the reasons for this extraordinary secrecy?'

The grey-haired lady said 'This is an extraordinary child. She has a neurological condition which, so far as I understand it, has not been come across before. I have given details of this condition in my own words in my report. She has an area in her brain the function of which seems to be to observe, scan, evaluate, what is being received by other areas of the brain, and then possibly to re-assess this. The technical language I'm afraid gets beyond me, but in any case the diagnosis is obviously to a large extent conjectural.'

The man in the centre of the row at the table looked

first one way, then the other; then down at the paper in front of him. He said 'Your concern is that this child should continue to live in circumstances in which this new growth and her special condition can continue to develop and to be observed and studied from time to time free from conditions and distractions which would inevitably disturb and distort the subject of such observation if she were in the public domain.'

The grey-haired lady said 'That is correct.'

'So it is to this end that it is necessary that she grows up in what might be called a natural even if unusual family environment, in order that her special condition may be of the greatest assistance to our scientific understanding of what might be a turn in human evolution. Whereas if she lived in the public eye with her unusual condition made public, she would inevitably be exposed to such intrusive enquiry that any fresh insight or understanding that might become available to us would be swamped by the well-known effects of such harassment.'

'That is correct.'

'The problem is, of course, that the style of what normally could be called a normal family environment is unlikely in this case to be what is required. A so-called 'normal' family nowadays is usually plagued by rivalries and possessiveness and deceits from which it might be hoped that one day we might be freed. This child shows signs, both neurological and behavioural, of being imbued with qualities free of such curses, which in the future might become of evolutionary advantage. What is required of us is to find an unusual family in which it might be possible for a new understanding to consider normal.'

Here the man at the centre of the table broke off and glared as if reprovingly, first at the papers in front of him and then to the left and right of him along the table. After a time he said 'Is that clear.'

After a slightly shorter pause someone along the table said 'Yes.'

The man looked up at the grey-haired woman in front of him. He said, as if with a struggle he might be suppressing amusement – 'And you say you think you may have found such a family.'

The grey-haired lady said 'Yes.'

The man said 'Abnormal: potentially normal.'

'Yes.'

One of the women along the table lowered her head onto her hands in front of her.

The grey-haired lady went on – 'This is a family of two women, two men, and two children. One of the women was made pregnant by one of the men and they married. Then some time later she left him to live with the other man, taking with her the child, while the first man went travelling to do scientific neurological research. All this occurred at the choice and with the encouragement of all concerned. In the course of his experiences, he whom we have called the first man found himself looking for her who can now hopefully be called the second woman, who had been a charity worker in East Africa and who with the brief help of the second man had rescued from a refugee camp the child who is now the subject of our report. I am afraid this is unlikely to be very clear; and indeed it has become hugely obscured by attempts to make it conform to what might seem understandable in the hysterical eyes of contemporary society. But yes, this is why we hope to avoid publicity. The couple who are not in law married, but who live with the child of the other man as if they are, now have their own child, a girl, and will be joined, I trust soon, by the man and the woman who are returning from East Africa where they met while each was researching the background of the child in whom each in his own way had taken a dedicated interest. Also, I trust, if this meeting is successful, they will be joined by the girl who is the subject of our discussion, now ten or eleven years old. And for her, all four adults will accept responsibility.'

The woman who had had her head on her hands on the table looked up at the ceiling and said 'And you say these people have no envies nor resentments nor deceits.'

The grey-haired lady said 'They will have had the practice of having a chance of being a prototype of a new brand of family,'

'Which may change the world.'

The grey-haired lady said nothing.

Someone said 'Where are they in fact now?'

Someone else said 'Does that matter? In fact surely that is just what we are being told people should not concern themselves with.'

The grey-haired lady said 'Look, there's a way in which none of our discussion here matters. We all know that if any evolutionary development of the human mind, the human personality, is to happen, then it is likely to occur by so-called chance. But then if it is to be nurtured, to flourish instead of to be snuffed out, this will depend on the environment, the soil as it were, in which the seed has landed – and either will or will not be able to take root. The exact style of such an environment, and such a process, can hardly be put into precise words, it has to be experienced. I have done my best to explore what and where I can.'

After another silence someone said 'So what you're saying to us is – either we trust you or we don't.'

The grey-haired lady said 'Yes.' Then – 'And I suppose trust is the hope of the whole experiment.'

Someone else said 'You mean trust in something that science can't explain.'

The grey-haired lady said 'I suppose so.'

Someone else said 'Can we meet the child?'

The man at the middle of the group behind the table said 'For God's sake no! I should be terrified of doing or saying something inappropriate!'

The grey-haired lady said 'But when people are in the presence of this child they are not made uneasy. They say they have the impression that she is in contact with something – is aware of the presence of things – of which they and we are not. But with her perhaps we may be. And God knows this may not be unscientific, with all the myriad dimensions and even universes that scientists cannot see or explain but which they say are pressing round us.'

And then it was as if no one had anything more to say.

*

Johnny and Joanna were sitting side by side on the floor with their backs against the wall of an airport departure area in which children were playing around and over-somnolent grown-ups reclining on benches or on bits of clothing on the floor. Joanna had her head resting on Johnny's shoulder. Johnny was saying 'Why do you think she might not accept you, she's my wife.'

Joanna said 'Exactly.'

Johnny said 'But it's not exactly. You could hardly get anything more paradoxical.'

'That's what I meant.'

'Oh I see.'

Johnny looked around as if he were a stammerer looking for a sayable word. Then he said 'What exactly did the hospital say.'

Joanna said 'They said it wasn't the hydrocephalus now, it was more like the rudiments or vestiges of another brain.'

Johnny said 'You see – '

'What?'

'No not see. But they'll let us take her.'

'They can't not. That's what you mean, isn't it?'

'You mean when it's both/and rather than either/or, there isn't a choice.'

'Yes.'

'I didn't know you'd be so clever.'

He was thinking – Then isn't it a wonder one can say anything at all! Then – I wonder how Peter is getting on with his stammer.

She said 'Stop it.' Then – 'And I'm not what's called clever.'

A rubber ball landed at his feet and Johnny picked it up and threw it high into the air and shouted 'Catch it!'

She said 'Could one part of the brain really be aware of what might be going on in another dimension, and inform the rest of the brain?'

Johnny said 'It wouldn't feel like that.'

She said 'But other people would be aware of it?'

Johnny said 'I don't see why not.'

*

From the window of a bungalow with a veranda and corrugated iron roof and wooden walls raised on blocks of stone now hidden under water, a man looked out on a scene which seemed to be a sea awash with flotsam. This consisted mostly of the material of what had once been small semi-circular tents. Around and beside these people up to their knees in water tugged, without much apparent success, at whatever they could lay their hands on. It was not clear if they were trying to save their belongings or themselves. The man at the window said 'And this is officially a drought.'

A woman sitting in the room behind him at a table in front of an old-fashioned computer said 'Well it seems they get things wrong for a purpose nowadays.'

The man said 'Well if you know this, you've got a chance of getting it right.'

The woman said 'I don't know.'

After a pause in which the man seemed to be

looking round for a word by which he would not stammer, he said 'You said you knew the woman.'

The woman said 'I said I knew she used to work here.'

'How did she know about the plane?'

'Know about what plane?'

'All right, the fuselage. You knew it had been booby trapped.'

'No.'

'It was to discourage looters.'

'Well it didn't, did it.'

'You mean they pinched the booby traps.' The man seemed to be struggling again, this time not to laugh.

The woman pushed the computer away from her and closed her eyes as if she were exhausted. After a time she said 'All right, you know they say the man was a government agent.'

The man behind her said 'And you knew he wasn't?'

'That's what I'm saying.'

'Then why don't you say it?'

The woman banged her fist down on the keys of the computer so that several of them jammed. She said 'All right, it's all my fault.'

The man said 'Yes isn't that what we're all supposed to be saying.'

The woman said 'What?'

The man said 'That once you've said that, there's hope.'

The woman said 'All right. How did they get through so easily?'

The man said 'They say that the thing about the baby is that things seem to happen quite naturally.'

'But they hadn't found the baby.'

'No they were looking for it.'

After another silence the woman said 'Oh all right, I've said all right, what woman, what man, what baby?'

The man said 'Anyway, they say she's an eleven-year-old girl now.'

The woman said 'That's better.'

*

Peter came home from school that afternoon with his jacket slung over his shoulder and looking pleased with himself. I was in the front garden keeping an eye on the lane. I said 'Have you been fighting?' Peter said 'No, playing.' I said 'What?' He said 'Someone said you weren't married to my mother.'

'And what did you say?'

'I said – No, my father's married to my mother.'

'That was clever.'

Peter said 'I think they're jealous.'

'What of?'

'I tell them they should love their enemies.'

'And what do they say?'

'What does that mean?'

'And what do you say?'

Peter said, 'You can't put it into words. You do it and then it happens.'

I wanted to laugh, but tears came into my eyes.

Alix put her head out of a first floor window. She said 'They're on their way.' Then – 'But where will we all sleep?'

I said 'I told you, Johnny's being lent a caravan.'

Alix said 'But tonight?'

Phoebe came running out of the house. She said 'She can come in with me!'

Peter said 'And there's room in my tent for Dad.'

Phoebe said 'But I know she'll come in with me!'

And Alix said with one of her smiles 'And Joanna can come in with me.'

It was a clear cloudless sky, so there were no bars to stop anything or anyone floating down from above.

Peter was saying 'What does she look like?'

I was saying 'I haven't seen her since she was a few days old.'

'And she's not my father's baby?'

'Not in that sense, no.'

Phoebe said 'She's all of our baby.'

I was thinking – This is like learning a new language. Yes.

Peter said 'She's different.'

I said 'Maybe.'

'Will we one day all become like her?'

'We may do, I don't know.'

Phoebe was saying 'But she'll know me!'

I was saying 'Yes I'm sure.'

Peter was saying 'But who's her mummy then?'

I said 'Her mummy died.'

Phoebe said 'We're all her mummy.'

I thought – But it doesn't matter if we know we sometimes get the languages muddled.

Peter said 'Who's the lady who's coming with Daddy then?'

Phoebe said 'She's called Joanna.'

I said 'She's a lady I met some time ago, when we found the baby.'

Peter said 'But then hasn't Daddy found the baby?'

I said 'Yes.'

Phoebe said 'But now she's found us!'

I said 'That's right.'

There had been times in the last few days when in response to Peter's and Phoebe's questions I had wondered if I should go into longer and more detailed explanations. But then I had thought – There are no detailed explanations, you have to come into knowledge of such things for yourself.

I said 'You won't ask too many questions, will you?'

Peter said 'No, we've promised.'

Phoebe said 'Look, there's a car!'

We were in the small front garden of the cottage behind the low stone wall and the rickety gate. We had got out of the house just to be in the open air, I think; or as I now put it – To be open to the air. Or were we like soldiers who have done whatever they had to do and so have now left their shelter to make peace? The car was coming bumping down the track from the harbour; in it there were only two people in the front, neither of them was Joanna; or was it she who was driving? – You mean, we are now indistinguishable? The car had stopped, and Johnny was getting out of the driver's door and coming round the front. The whole situation now seemed to be happening both here and in front of some audience. Johnny was saying 'What a place to find, like that moon of Pluto or the source of the Nile!' I was opening the passenger door for the girl. I said 'Welcome.' The girl said 'Thank you.' Alix came forward and as soon as the girl was out of the car Alix put her hands on her shoulders and gave her a kiss. The girl stood quietly. Phoebe came and stood beside Alix and said 'I'm Phoebe.' The girl said 'Hullo Phoebe.' Then the girl turned to Peter and said 'And you're Peter?' Peter said 'Hullo.' She was a fine figure of a girl, with sun-tanned skin and dark hair – very arresting. Alix said 'Come in and have some tea.' Then to Johnny 'Where's Joanna?' Johnny said 'She was feeling a bit over the odds, so she thought she'd walk the last half mile.' I thought – Or she might already be in the kitchen having tea.

When Joanna did arrive she looked tired and somewhat ravaged, so the one comfortable chair was found for her, and it was accepted that she would not want to talk. It struck me – Yes of course, when you have climbed the tree of knowledge of good and evil, and have eaten the fruit, you have absolved your enemies. The girl was sitting between Peter and Phoebe. I thought – We must give her a name. I said 'You know us all now. If there's anything you want or need, just let us know.' She said 'Thank you.' And then to me 'I did know you, didn't I?' I said 'Yes.' Joanna said 'We were together just after I found you.' The girl said 'What were you going to call me?' Peter said 'Metamorphosis.' Phoebe said 'And I'm Sis!'

ENVOI

The girl we called Jenny came running down the hill so fast that it was as if with the wind behind her she might be picked up and wafted over the rocks and into the sea. And then it would be as if she had been flying.

I said 'What's wrong!'

She said 'Nothing!' Then – 'I think I got it.' She stood still, looking out to sea.

She sometimes seemed to hear something, to be watching something, that was both herself and other than herself, as if she were in two places at the same time.

She said 'There was a man in a car on the road and he stopped and offered me a lift and anything else I would like, ice-creams and so on.' She laughed.

'And what did you say?'

'I told him that if he lay down on his back on the road I'd shit into his mouth, if that's what he'd like.'

'And what did he say?'

'He made a grab at me. Then I got away.'

'How?'

'I don't know. I hit him with a brick I think.'

I said 'And where did you get that stuff about shit?'

'I think it was something I heard Joanna once say.

About human nature.'

I said 'What?'

'That it was part of it.'

'How?'

'I don't know.'

She remained staring out to sea. I thought – It's not possible to know?

I said 'We'd better get back to the house.'

She said 'Yes.' Then on the way she said 'Roots are underground.'

I said 'Yes.' I thought – And our heads are in the clouds?

Then she stopped and said 'I'd better go and see if things are all right.'

I said 'What, the man?'

She said 'Yes.' Then – 'Things can grow, change, can't they?'

I thought – You mean, we come into the world usually upside down?

She said 'Wasn't that what you were talking about the other day?'

I was thinking – no not thinking – being aware of things floating into my head like bubbles and bursting there like rain – Well what do you do about evil; were we not given choice? How can there be choice without evil as well as good; but still, there are the assurances for good? If there are any bricks lying around, all right –

But Jenny was running off again, round the brow of the hill towards where the road passed by the farm buildings, which were indeed being rebuilt.

And what was that other thing I had been talking about with Johnny the other day? There had been that man I had met who had said to me – Do you know why we're in Afghanistan? And I had said – Yes, to keep the heroin trade going. And Johnny had said – Were the Taleban really stopping it?

And I was thinking now – Yes, this has got to do with that.

In the cottage Johnny was sitting with his feet propped up on the window sill and a newspaper held in front of him as if to protect him from the light. He spoke as if he were quoting from the newspaper.

'Cosmologists are now saying that the universe is a hologram of processes on the surface of a two dimensional sphere.'

Peter said 'That's a spoof.'

Joanna said 'Not clever enough to be a spoof.'

Alix said 'Dark matter and dark energy aren't clever.'

Johnny said 'No.'

I thought – You mean –

Phoebe said 'I'm trying to do my homework.'

Peter got up and went out of the door which led to the scullery and then to the back garden and, if one so wished, to the farm buildings.

I said 'What were we saying the other day when we were talking about how to love one's enemies?'

Johnny said 'When was that?'

I said 'Do you offer to give them what they want?'

Alix said 'It's not impossible, they want to die.'

Phoebe pushed away the notebook on the table in front of her and said 'There, that's done.'

Johnny said 'We all might do a bit of homework.'

Alix said 'Yes.'

Peter came back through the door from the scullery and the garden. He was followed by Jenny. Jenny said 'Can I do a bit?'

Alix said 'Yes.'

Jenny sat in a chair across the table from me. Peter said 'There's a man on the floor in the cowshed. He says a brick fell on his head.'

Jenny said 'You say you just found me. Came across me'

Joanna said 'Yes.'

Jenny said 'What else?'

I said 'There was some inevitability about it.'

Jenny said 'In what way?'

Peter said 'In a refugee camp, in East Africa.'

Johnny said 'Why were you there?'

Joanna said 'More than that.'

I said 'Yes.'

Jenny said 'What was particular about me?'

Joanna said 'We didn't know.'

I said 'We had the experience.'

Jenny said 'And that was that?'

Joanna said 'Yes.'

Peter said 'But what about you.'

Jenny looked at him. She said, as if inevitably – 'Yes.'

Peter said 'But have you got something particular to do?'

Jenny said 'I don't know.'

I thought – There was that time in Jerusalem when that girl came into the café and held out to me her clenched fist as if to drop from it something into the open palms of my hands. And then, when she left, the bomb went off just outside.

Jenny said to me 'I meant, what you said you had been saying about your time in Jerusalem.'

I thought 'Yes, but that was about how on earth does one love those who evidently are one's enemies.'

Then – 'But what on earth has this got to do with the man in the cowshed?'

Jenny said 'Yes.'

Johnny said 'It needn't mean stopping them being enemies.'

Jenny said 'No.'

Joanna said 'But what about the man in the cowshed?'

I wanted to say – You know about the man in the cowshed?

Peter said 'He says he's been hit on the head by a brick.'

I wanted to say – I see.

Alix said 'They're doing building work in the cowshed.'

I said 'Yes.'

Jenny said 'But is he all right?'

Johnny said 'You can fight your enemies and love them at the same time.'

Peter said 'Yes.'

Alix said 'But does it work.'

I thought – Well we'll see.

A man appeared at the door from the scullery. He was fat and leathery. He said 'I just wanted to let you know I'm all right.' He was speaking as if to Jenny. Then he turned to the rest of us and said 'A brick fell from the ceiling.'

Jenny said 'It was lying by the side of the road.'

The man said 'Very handy.' He seemed to try to smile.

Alix was by the sink with her back to the room. She said 'You were talking about Jerusalem.'

I said 'You came out to look after me.'

Jenny said to the man 'Palestinians and Israelis.' Then – 'Thank you.'

The man said as if bewildered 'Oh I see.' Then he nodded, and disappeared back into the scullery and so, presumably, out of the back door and across the yard and on to the road. But how does one know?

Johnny said as if to Jenny 'So what about them?'

Peter said 'They don't love themselves.'

Alix said 'That's right.'

Phoebe said 'Homework's done.'

Jenny said 'That's right.'

Peter said 'What's so particular about Jerusalem?'

Johnny said 'Usually is.'

I said 'I was working on a film there. Which didn't work.'

Joanna said 'Oh but it did.'

Phoebe said 'I said, homework's done.'

*

I don't know when it began to be suspected by people who watched the news on television in order to find out what was happening in the world outside, that most of what was being shown was not in the context of true versus false, or right versus wrong, but more in the context of what would be entertaining, both for performers and viewers. This was sometimes made explicit, as for instance in a science programme in which a professional comic was brought in to act as 'front man' to a professor of quantum physics – the only way, it seemed to be assumed, by which an audience's attention might be held by the professor's admitted incomprehensibilities. And regarding matters of politics and economics, were not experts now openly admitting that there were no ultimate answers to such questions, but was it not still their job to try to show they were doing their best.

And in the commentary columns of newspapers there began to appear quite cool and calm recognition that all this might indeed herald some apocalypse in understanding; but then had not humans always felt some excitement or even relief at the prospect of calamity? In our quiet home in Ireland we seldom watched the television except for the news or for sport; but then usually with the sound turned off, so that one had the chance of making one's own assessment about style and significance. Sometimes Peter would ask Johnny or me questions about current affairs, and sometimes we would ask Peter questions about sport. And sometimes I would think about asking Jenny questions about meaning; but I knew that she would know that we would be groping for answers beyond words.

Joanna said 'You mean, all this is how things are supposed to be?'

Alix said 'I mean, can't it be a game?'

Johnny said 'Indeed. Isn't apocalypse better as a game?'

Peter said 'I like games.'

Phoebe said 'Not higgledy piggledy.'

*

I asked Jenny to come with me into the town by the harbour to do some shopping. I thought it might be easier to talk with just the two of us in the car. I had once driven into the town with Peter, when he had wanted to know what was meant by the tree of knowledge of good and evil in the Garden of Eden story: was this knowledge that of the evident difference between good and evil, or of their possible interconnectedness? And it had seemed that there were not exact answers to these questions, except that this and that had then happened.

As Jenny and I came down from the green hills to the harbour there were small fishing boats either moored to buoys or lying on their sides on the mud. Jenny said 'What did people mean by an eye for an eye and a tooth for a tooth; that right and wrong had to balance mathematically?'

I said 'Except that mathematics don't seem to balance, they seem to go on for ever.'

She said 'Yes.'

I said 'But there is a structure, to consider this.'

She said 'To choose.'

I said 'Yes, but not necessarily between one or the other, but the chance of both at the same time.'

She said 'And then this or that happens.'

I said 'Yes.'

I stopped the car. It was sometimes difficult to know just where one was with Jenny. There had come into my mind that time in Jerusalem when I was on the outskirts of the city walking between the high walls which had been put up to ensure separation like imprisonment. And a woman had come out of a heavily barred doorway and had held out towards me a bundle which looked as if it might contain a baby. But before I had had time to consider whether to take it in my arms, some armed men appeared from behind me and pushed the woman with the bundle back through the doorway, and then slammed the door shut and re-bolted it. When they then turned to me I stood still and did nothing. And after a time they moved away. At least this is how I remembered it. Jenny was now climbing out of the car and squatting on her haunches at the edge of the pavement and holding her hand out as if to a dog. She said 'There was a dog, wasn't there?'

I said 'Yes, it was hungry, and was trying to take food from an old woman's basket. So we took it home and looked after it and fed it, for some days, until eventually its owner came for it.'

Jenny said 'But you did look after it.'

I said 'Yes.' It seemed then that I was back in Jerusalem and tears were about to come into my eyes. I said 'We had been wondering whether or not to stay on here.'

Jenny said 'And you did.'

I said 'Yes.'

I thought – Peter might have told her the story.

It now appeared that I had stopped the car in front of the door of the house from which, when I had been with Peter, the man had appeared with what had seemed to be a gun, or perhaps the handle of a broom.

Jenny was still holding her hand out towards the house. Then the door opened and the man that I remembered appeared, and smiled at Jenny. He said 'Do you want your doggie back?'

Jenny said 'It isn't ours.'

The man said 'No?'

Jenny said 'I just wanted to say Hullo.'

The man said 'Hullo then.'

The dog that Phoebe had called Smelly, because it had so much liked sniffing her, now came out of the doorway and went up to Jenny and licked her hand.

Jenny said 'The same to you.'

An old woman – I was not sure that she was the

old woman who had been pushing the shopping basket that the dog had tried to take things from, but she surely could have been – now appeared in the doorway beside the man, and held out a large dish of dog-food towards the dog and Jenny. The dog left Jenny and followed the old woman with the food back into the house. The man was saying to me 'They haven't been troubling you then.'

I said 'No.'

He said 'Let me know if they do.'

I said 'I will.'

I thought – He is a Mr Brewster who keeps the peace between the loyalists and republicans?

There had been news on the television recently of new disturbances in Belfast. Someone had hung a flag or something at an inappropriate time or place or angle. Then things had calmed down.

Jenny had got back into the car. We waved goodbye.

Jenny said 'We haven't done any shopping.'

I said 'No.'

Jenny said 'Yes.'

As we drove up the bumpy road from the harbour to the smooth green slopes that led to the cliff-tops, I was thinking – So what do we see – that we may not have to worry about Jerusalem after all because things there, after how many thousands of years, may be with this vision sorting themselves out? I mean the realisation of what is, or what is not, if one doesn't see it, a game. And also in this part of the world in which we happen to have settled – what – a lament for – what is it – 'Oh my grief, I've lost him surely, I've lost the only playboy in the western world!'

Jenny was now saying 'What was that about trouble?'

I was thinking – Oh but Jenny, aren't you telling me?

I said 'The troubles between the North and the South seemed to be having another bit of a flare-up, but now with luck it may be seen to be more of a game.'

Jenny said 'So that's all right?'

I said 'Don't you think?'

Jenny said 'I don't know.'

When we got home there was more news on television about the flag that had been flown upside down or whatever; but also news about the planned talks between Israelis and Palestinians in danger of once more being postponed because of the new threat of rockets being launched and hitting a target here or there at the press of a distant button – this offering an excuse for more houses to be squeezed into spaces already like a prison.

Johnny said 'There's also news that if it never stops

raining, there'll be another flood like that of Noah.'

Joanna said 'I thought this time the flood was seen to be of words.'

Alix said 'Well we've got our ark all ready.'

Peter said 'Would we take any animals?'

Phoebe said 'Lovely smelly animals.'

Jenny sat with her back to the fire staring down at the palms of her hands held open on her knees. I wondered – What does she think might drop into them?

I said to Johnny 'There seems to have been talk about us in the town.'

Johnny said 'Well, there would be, wouldn't there.'

Alix said 'They seem to like what we've done with the buildings.'

Joanna said 'Isn't it about what we might be doing?'

Jenny said 'Is it true, or is it a story, that one can now contrive a means by which one can put out of action all computers and their attachments at almost any distance?'

Peter said 'Would you want that?'

Jenny said 'I don't know.'

Johnny said 'It may be true in theory.'

Joanna said 'How could they test it?'

Alix said 'It could be a game?'

I thought – Who on earth would risk it?

Then – Oh well, perhaps God. For another Noah?

Then in my mind I thought I heard a rifle shot

outside; but I had thought I heard something like this once before, and had I not explained it as the disturbance of air by something passing harmlessly overhead?

But Peter said 'What was that?'

And Jenny said 'I'll go and see.'

Joanna said 'No you've done enough.'

Johnny said 'I'd like to say I'm sorry.'

Alix said 'You've said it.'

I was thinking – I mean, if the consequence of knowledge of good and evil is that we become like gods, then how does it matter if we also die? Would not that seem also good? Do not gods die –

Because otherwise how could one stand it.

I mean gods of course also do not die –

Or how could one understand it.

Joanna was saying 'Not in words.'

Alix said 'Not in trying not to be like animals.'

Phoebe said 'Lovely smelly human beings.'

Peter said 'Game means – Spirited, Willing – I looked it up.'

Jenny said as if to Phoebe or herself – 'Not higgledy piggledy?'

I thought – And Peter no longer stammers!

Phoebe said 'Why not higgledy piggledy; that's not a game, it's a dance!'

We gazed at her.

I thought – I know! I'll take the children down to the beach tomorrow and we'll watch the sea and the clouds and the sky.

SELECTED DALKEY ARCHIVE TITLES

MICHAL AJVAZ, *The Golden Age.*
The Other City.

PIERRE ALBERT-BIROT, *Grabinoulor.*

YUZ ALESHKOVSKY, *Kangaroo.*

FELIPE ALFAU, *Chromos.*
Locos.

IVAN ÂNGELO, *The Celebration.*
The Tower of Glass.

ANTÓNIO LOBO ANTUNES,
Knowledge of Hell.
The Splendor of Portugal.

ALAIN MRIAS-MISSON,
Theatre of Incest.

JOHN ASHBERY AND
JAMES SCHUYLER,
A Nest of Ninnies.

ROBERT ASHLEY, *Perfect Lives.*

GABRIELA AVIGUR-ROTEM,
Heatwave and Crazy Birds.

DJUNA BARNES, *Ladies Almanack.*
Ryder.

JOHN BARTH, *Letters.*
Sabbatical.

DONALD BARTHELME, *The King.*
Paradise.

SVETISLAV BASARA, *Chinese Letter.*

MIQUEL BAUÇÀ, *The Siege in the Room.*

RENÉ BELLETTO, *Dying.*

MAREK BIEŃCZYK, *Transparency.*

ANDREI BITOV, *Pushkin House.*

ANDREJ BLATNIK, *You Do Understand.*

LOUIS PAUL BOON, *Chapel Road.*
My Little War.
Summer in Termuren.

ROGER BOYLAN, *Killoyle.*

IGNÁCIO DE LOYOLA BRANDÃO,
Anonymous Celebrity.
Zero.

BONNIE BREMSER,
Troia: Mexican Memoirs.

CHRISTINE BROOKE-ROSE,
Amalgamemnon.

BRIGID BROPHY, *In Transit.*

GERALD L. BRUNS,
Modern Poetry and the Idea of Language.

GABRIELLE BURTON, *Heartbreak Hotel.*

MICHEL BUTOR, *Degrees,*
Mobile.

G. CABRERA INFANTE,
Infante's Inferno.
Three Trapped Tigers.

JULIETA CAMPMPOS,
The Fear of Losing Eurydice.

ANNE CARSON, *Eros the Bittersweet.*

ORLY CASTEL-BLOOM, *Dolly City.*

LOUIS-FERDINAND CÉLINE,
Castle to Castle.
Conversations with Professor Y,
London Bridge,
Normance,
North,
Rigadoon.

MARIE CHAIX,
The Laurels of Lake Constance.

HUGO CHARTERIS, *The Tide Is Right.*

ERIC CHEVILLARD, *Demolishing Nisard.*

MARC CHOLODENKO, *Mordechai Schamz.*

JOSHUA COHEN, *Witz.*

SELECTED DALKEY ARCHIVE TITLES

EMILY HOLMES COLEMAN,
The Shutter of Snow.

ROBERT COOVER,
A Night at the Movies.

STANLEY CRAWFORD, *Log of the S.S,*
The Mrs Unguentine,
Some Instructions to My Wife.

RENÉ CREVEL, PUTTING
My Foot in It.

RALPH CUSACK, *Cadenza.*

NICHOLAS DELBANCO,
The Count of Concord,
Sherbrookes.

NIGEL DENNIS, *Cards of Identity.*

PETER DIMOCK,
A Short Rhetoric for Leaving the Family.

ARIEL DORFMFMAN, *Konfidenz.*

COLEMAN DOWELL, *Island People,*
Too Much Flesh and Jabez.

ARKADII DRAGOMOSHCHENKO,
Dust.

RIKKI DUCORNET,
The Complete Butcher's Tales,
The Fountains of Neptune,
The Jade Cabinet,
Phosphor in Dreamland.

WILLIAM EASTLAKE, *The Bamboo Bed,*
Castle Keep,
Lyric of the Circle Heart.

JEAN ECHENOZ, *Chopin's Move.*

STANLEY ELKIN, *A Bad Man,*
Criers and Kibitzers, Kibitzers and Criers,
The Dick Gibson Show,
The Franchiser,
The Living End,
Mrs. Ted Bliss.

FRANÇOIS EMMMMANUEL,
Invitation to a Voyage.

SALVADOR ESPRIU,
Ariadne in the Grotesque Labyrinth.

LESLIE A. FIEDLER,
Love and Death in the American Novel.

JUAN FILLOY, *Op Oloop.*

ANDY FITCH, *Pop Poetics.*

GUSTAVE FLAUBERT,
Bouvard and Pécuchet.

KASS FLEISHER, *Talking out of School.*

FORD MADOX FORD,
The March of Literature.

JON FOSSE, *Aliss at the Fire,*
Melancholy.

MAX FRISCH, *I'm Not Stiller,*
Man in the Holocene.

CARLOS FUENTES, *Christopher Unborn, Distant Relations, Terra Nostra,*
Where the Air Is Clear.

TAKEHIKO FUKUNAGA,
Flowers of Grass.

WILLIAM GADDIS, J R,
The Recognitions.

JANICE GALLOWAY, *Foreign Parts,*
The Trick Is to Keep Breathing.

WILLIAM H H. GASS,
Cartesian Sonata and Other Novellas,
Finding a Form,
A Temple of Texts,
The Tunnel,
Willie Masters' Lonesome Wife.

GÉRARD GAVARRY, *Hoppla! 1 2 3.*

ETIENNE GILSON,
The Arts of the Beautiful, Forms and Substances in the Arts.

SELECTED DALKEY ARCHIVE TITLES

C. S S. GISCOMBE,
Giscome Road, Here.

DOUGLAS GLOVER,
Bad News of the Heart.

WITOLD GOMBROWICZ,
A Kind of Testament.

PAULO EMÍLIO SALES GOMES,
P's Three Women.

GEORGI GOSPODINOV,
Natural Novel.

JUAN GOYTISOLO, *Count Julian,*
Juan the Landless,
Makbara,
Marks of Identity.

HENRY GREEN, *Back,*
Blindness,
Concluding,
Doting,
Nothing.

JACK GREEN, *Fire the Bastards!*

JIRˇI´ GRUSˇA, *The Questionnaire.*

MELA HARTWIG,
Am I a Redundant Human Being?

JOHN HAWKES, *The Passion Artist,*
Whistlejacket.

ELIZABETH HEIGHWAY, ED.,
Contemporary Georgian Fiction.

ALEKSANDAR HEMON, ED.,
Best European Fiction.

AIDAN HIGGINS, *Balcony of Europe,*
Blind Man's Bluff,
Bornholm Night-Ferry,
Flotsam and Jetsam,
Langrishe, Go Down,
Scenes from a Receding Past.

KEIZO HINO, *Isle of Dreams.*

KAZUSHI HOSAKA, *Plainsong.*

ALDOUS HUXLEY, *Antic Hay,*
Crome Yellow,
Point Counter Point,
Those Barren Leaves,
Time Must Have a Stop.

NAOYUKI II, *The Shadow of a Blue Cat.*

GERT JONKE, *The Distant Sound,*
Geometric Regional Novel,
Homage to Czerny,
The System of Vienna.

JACQUES JOUET, *Mountain R,*
Savage,
Upstaged.

MIEKO KANAI, *The Word Book.*

YORAM KANIUK, *Life on Sandpaper.*

HUGH KENNER, Flaubert,
Joyce and Beckett: The Stoic Comedians,
Joyce's Voices.

DANILO KISˇ, *The Attic,*
Garden, Ashes,
The Lute and the Scars,
Psalm 44,
A Tomb for Boris Davidovich.

ANITA KONKKA, *A Fool's Paradise.*

GEORGE KONRÁD, *The City Builder.*

TADEUSZ KONWICKI,
A Minor Apocalypse,
The Polish Complex.

MENIS KOUMANDAREAS, *Koula.*

ELAINE KRAF,
The Princess of 72nd Street.

JIM KRUSOE, *Iceland.*

AYŞE KULIN,
Farewell: A Mansion in Occupied
Istanbul.

FOR A FULL LIST OF PUBLICATIONS, VISIT: www.dalkeyarchive.com

SELECTED DALKEY ARCHIVE TITLES

EMILIO LASCANO TEGUI, *On Elegance While Sleeping.*

ERIC LAURRENT, *Do Not Touch.*

VIOLETTE LEDUC, *La Bâtarde.*

EDOUARD LEVÉ, *Autoportrait, Suicide.*

MARIO LEVI, *Istanbul Was a Fairy Tale.*

DEBORAH LEVY, *Billy and Girl.*

JOSE´ LEZAMA LIMA, *Paradiso.*

ROSA LIKSOM, *Dark Paradise.*

OSMAN LINS, *Avalovara, The Queen of the Prisons of Greece.*

ALF MAC LOCHLAINN, *The Corpus in the Library, Out of Focus.*

RON LOEWINSOHN, *Magnetic Field(s).*

MINA LOY, *Stories and Essays of Mina Loy.*

D. KEITH MANO, *Take Five.*

MICHELINE AHARONIAN MARCOM, *The Mirror in the Well.*

BEN MARCUS, *The Age of Wire and String.*

WALLACE MARKFIELD, *Teitlebaum's Window, To an Early Grave.*

DAVID MARKSON, *Reader's Block, Wittgenstein's Mistress.*

CAROLE MASO, *AVA.*

LADISLAV MATEJKA & KRYSTYNA POMORSKA, EDS., *Readings in Russian Poetics: Formalist and Structuralist Views.*

HARRY MATHEWS, *Cigarettes, The Conversions, The Human Country: New and Collected Stories, The Journalist, My Life in CIA, Singular Pleasures, The Sinking of the Odradek Stadium, Tlooth.*

JOSEPH MCELROY, *Night Soul and Other Stories.*

ABDELWAHAB MEDDEB, *Talismano.*

GERHARD MEIER, *Isle of the Dead.*

HERMAN MELVILLE, *The Confidence-Man.*

AMANDA MICHALOPOULOU, *I'd Like.*

STEVEN MILLHAUSER, *The Barnum Museum, In the Penny Arcade.*

RALPH J. MILLS, JR., *Essays on Poetry.*

MOMUS, *The Book of Jokes.*

OLIVE MOORE, *Spleen.*

NICHOLAS MOSLEY, *Accident, Assassins, Catastrophe Practice, Experience and Religion, A Garden of Trees, Hopeful Monsters, Imago Bird, Impossible Object, Inventing God, Judith, Look at the Dark, Natalie Natalia, Serpent, Time at War.*

FOR A FULL LIST OF PUBLICATIONS, VISIT: www.dalkeyarchive.com

SELECTED DALKEY ARCHIVE TITLES

CHRISTINE MONTALBETTI,
The Origin of Man,
Western.

WARREN MOTTE, *Fables of the Novel: French Fiction since 1990,*
Fiction Now: The French Novel in the 21st Century,
Oulipo: A Primer of Potential Literature.

GERALD MURNANE,
Barley Patch, Inland.

YVES NAVARRE,
Our Share of Time,
Sweet Tooth.

DOROTHY NELSON, *In Night's City,*
Tar and Feathers.

ESHKOL NEVO, *Homesick.*

WILFRIDO D D. NOLLEDO,
But for the Lovers.

FLANN O'BRIEN, *At Swim-Two-Birds,*
The Best of Myles,
The Dalkey Archive,
The Hard Life,
The Poor Mouth,
The Third Policeman.

CLAUDE OLLIER, *The Mise-en-Scène,*
Wert and the Life Without End.

GIOVANNI ORELLI, *Walaschek's Dream.*

PATRIK OUŘEDNÍK, *Europeana,*
The Opportune Moment, 1855.

BORIS PAHOR, *Necropolis.*

FERNANDO DEL PASO,
News from the Empire,
Palinuro of Mexico.

ROBERT PINGET, *The Inquisitory,*
Mahu or The Material,
Trio.

MANUEL PUIG,
Betrayed by Rita Hayworth,
The Buenos Aires Affair,
Heartbreak Tango.

RAYMYMOND QUENEAU,
The Last Days, Odile,
Pierrot Mon Ami,
Saint Glinglin.

ANN QUIN, *Berg,*
Passages,
Three,
Tripticks.

ISHMAEL REED,
The Free-Lance Pallbearers,
The Last Days of Louisiana Red,
Ishmael Reed: The Plays,
Juice!,
Reckless Eyeballing,
The Terrible Threes,
The Terrible Twos,
Yellow Back Radio Broke-Down.

JASIA REICHARDT,
15 Journeys Warsaw to London.

NOËLLE REVAZ,
With the Animals.

JOÃO UBALDO RIBEIRO,
House of the Fortunate Buddhas.

JEAN RICARDOU, *Place Names.*

RAINER MARIA RILKE,
The Notebooks of Malte Laurids Brigge.

JULIÁN RÍOS, *The House of Ulysses,*
Larva: A Midsummer Night's Babel,
Poundemonium,
Procession of Shadows.

AUGUSTO ROA BASTOS, *I the Supreme.*

DANIËL ROBBERECHTS,
Arriving in Avignon.

SELECTED DALKEY ARCHIVE TITLES

JEAN ROLIN,
The Explosion of the Radiator Hose.

OLIVIER ROLIN, *Hotel Crystal.*

ALIX CLEO ROUBAUD, *Alix's Journal.*

JACQUES ROUBAUD,
The Form of a City Changes Faster, Alas, Than the Human Heart,
The Great Fire of London,
Hortense in Exile,
Hortense Is Abducted,
The Loop,
Mathematics, The Plurality of Worlds of Lewis, The Princess Hoppy,
Some Thing Black.

RAYMYMOND ROUSSEL,
Impressions of Africa.

VEDRANA RUDAN, *Night.*

STIG SÆTERBAKKEN, *Siamese, Self Control.*

LYDIE SALVAYRE,
The Company of Ghosts,
The Lecture,
The Power of Flies.

LUIS RAFAEL SÁNCHEZ,
Macho Camacho's Beat.

SEVERO SARDUY, *Cobra & Maitreya.*

NATHALIE SARRAUTE,
Do You Hear Them?,
Martereau,
The Planetarium.

ARNO SCHMIDT, *Collected Novellas,*
Collected Stories,
Nobodaddy's Children.
Two Novels.

ASAF SCHURR, *Motti.*

GAIL SCOTT, *My Paris.*

DAMION SEARLS, *What We Were Doing and Where We Were Going.*

JUNE AKERS SEESE,
Is This What Other Women Feel Too?,
What Waiting Really Means.

BERNARD SHARE, *Inish, Transit.*

VIKTOR SHKLOVSKY, *Bowstring,*
Knight's Move,
A Sentimental Journey: Memoirs 1917–1922,
Energy of Delusion: A Book on Plot,
Literature and Cinematography,
Theory of Prose,
Third Factory,
Zoo, or Letters Not about Love.

PIERRE SINIAC, *The Collaborators.*

KJERSTI A. SKOMSVOLD,
The Faster I Walk,the Smaller I Am.

JOSEF SˇKVORECKY´,
The Engineer of Human Souls.

GILBERT SORRENTINO,
Aberration of Starlight,
Blue Pastoral,
Crystal Vision,
Imaginative Qualities of Actual Things,
Mulligan Stew,
Pack of Lies,
Red the Fiend,
The Sky Changes,
Something Said,
Splendide-Hôtel,
Steelwork,
Under the Shadow.

W. M. SPACKMAN, *The Complete Fiction.*

ANDRZEJ STASIUK, *Dukla,*
Fado.

FOR A FULL LIST OF PUBLICATIONS, VISIT: www.dalkeyarchive.com

SELECTED DALKEY ARCHIVE TITLES

GERTRUDE STEIN, *The Making of Americans, A Novel of Thank You.*

LARS SVENDSEN, *A Philosophy of Evil.*

PIOTR SZEWC, *Annihilation.*

GONÇALO M. TAVARES, *Jerusalem,*
Joseph Walser's Machine,
Learning to Pray in the Age of Technique.

LUCIAN DAN TEODOROVICI,
Our Circus Presents . . .

NIKANOR TERATOLOGEN,
Assisted Living.

STEFAN THEMERSON,
Hobson's Island,
The Mystery of the Sardine,
Tom Harris.

TAEKO TOMIOKA, *Building Waves.*

JOHN TOOMEY, *Sleepwalker.*

JEAN-PHILIPPPPE TOUSSAINT,
The Bathroom,
Camera,
Monsieur,
Reticence,
Running Away,
Self-Portrait Abroad,
Television,
The Truth about Marie.

DUMITRU TSEPENEAG,
Hotel Europa,
The Necessary Marriage,
Pigeon Post,
Vain Art of the Fugue.

ESTHER TUSQUETS,
Stranded.

DUBRAVKA UGRESIC,
Lend Me Your Character,
Thank You for Not Reading.

TOR ULVEN, *Replacement.*

MATI UNT,
Brecht at Night,
Diary of a Blood Donor,
Things in the Night.

ÁLVARO URIBE AND OLIVIA SEARS, EDS.,
Best of Contemporary Mexican Fiction.

ELOY URROZ, *Friction,*
The Obstacles.

LUISA VALENZUELA,
Dark Desires and the Others,
He Who Searches.

PAUL VERHAEGHEN,
Omega Minor.

AGLAJA VETERANYI,
Why the Child Is Cooking in the Polenta.

BORIS VIAN, *Heartsnatcher.*

LLORENÇ VILLALONGA,
The Dolls' Room.

TOOMAS VINT, *An Unending Landscape.*

ORNELA VORPSI,
The Country Where No One Ever Dies.

AUSTRYN WAINHOUSE,
Hedyphagetica.

CURTIS WHITE,
America's Magic Mountain,
The Idea of Home,
Memories of My Father Watching TV,
Requiem.

DIANE WILLIAMS,
Excitability: Selected Stories,
Romancer Erector.

DOUGLAS WOOLF,
Wall to Wall,
Ya! & John-Juan.

SELECTED DALKEY ARCHIVE TITLES

JAY WRIGHT,
Polynomials and Pollen,
The Presentable Art of Reading Absence.

PHILIP WYLIE, *Generation of Vipers.*

MARGUERITE YOUNG,
Angel in the Forest,
Miss MacIntosh, My Darling.

REYOUNG, *Unbabbling.*

VLADO ŽABOT, *The Succubus.*

ZORAN ŽIVKOVIĆ, *Hidden Camera.*

LOUIS ZUKOFSKY, *Collected Fiction.*

VITOMIL ZUPAN, *Minuet for Guitar.*

SCOTT ZWIREN, *God Head.*

FOR A FULL LIST OF PUBLICATIONS, VISIT: www.dalkeyarchive.com